REUNION AT COTTONWOOD STATION

REUNION AT COTTONWOOD STATION

A Western Quartet

T. T. FLYNN

Five Star • Waterville, Maine

First Edition
First Printing: July 2003

Published in 2003 in conjunction with
Golden West Literary Agency.

Set in 11 pt. Plantin by Minnie B. Raven.

Printed in the United States on permanent paper.

Library of Congress Cataloging-in-Publication Data

Flynn, T. T.
     Reunion at Cottonwood Station : a western quartet /
by T.T. Flynn.
          p. cm.
     "Five Star western"—T.p. verso.
     Contents: Brothers of the owlhoot—Rodeo's "A" man—
Outlawed—Reunion at Cottonwood Station.
     ISBN 0-7862-3787-2 (hc : alk. paper)
     1. Western stories. I. Title.
PS3556.L93R48 2003
813'.54—dc21   2002044758

REUNION AT COTTONWOOD STATION

Table of Contents

Brothers of the Owlhoot

T. T. Flynn completed the story he titled "Brothers of the Owlhoot" on December 31, 1934. Early in the new year it was sold to Rogers Terrill, editor of *Dime Western* at Popular Publications, for $500. *Dime Western* for a brief period—beginning with the issue dated 9/1/34 through the issue dated 11/15/35—was published twice a month. With the issue dated 12/1/35 it reverted to being a monthly magazine. This story was showcased in first position on the cover when it appeared under this same title in *Dime Western* (5/15/35).

I

Tam Matson was six years old when his brother John left the Coffee Pot range and took the outlaw trail. As the years passed and the fame of Red John Matson spread, young Tam heard and gloried in it. It was no matter to him that Red John was never mentioned at home, or that stern old Jeremiah Matson publicly declared that his son John was a son no longer. Red John was a hero to Tam Matson and his boyhood friends.

If the taciturn, bearded father had known that the favorite game of his remaining son was playing outlaw, punishment would have been swift and certain. But he never knew, nor did he ever hear of what happened that memorable night in Tam's twelfth year.

Riding home from Las Cabras under a white full moon, Tam met half a dozen mounted men. They stopped, began asking questions about Las Cabras. They wanted to know what strangers were in town, what the sheriff was doing, what the town talk was about. Tam knew they were outlaws. In the silver moonlight he could see every man heavily armed, unshaven, powdered with grayish alkali dust from hard riding. But he sat sideways in his saddle and answered the questions easily, and presently he calmly made a statement of his own.

"Red John Matson's my brother. Any of you know him?"

The nearest man uttered a soft oath, reined over close. "What's your name, kid?" he gruffly questioned.

"Tam Matson."

A match flared close to Tam's face. Blinking, he looked through the flickering light, saw a hard, clear-cut face that stirred dim memory.

Tam faltered: "You . . . you look like Johnny. The one I asked you about."

"You're crazy!" The match went out. Then suddenly the man's voice changed. A big arm reached out and grabbed Tam around the shoulder. "It's me, kid," said the voice in a way Tam never forgot, so warm and hungry and shaken was it. "I'm Johnny. Lord, you're sproutin' up fast, ain't you?"

There under the still white moon, with the low sagebrush spreading in dark waves to the far hills, Tam came for a moment close to his older brother. Like called to like in that moment—blood to blood.

"Why'n't you come home tonight, Johnny?" Tam begged, but he knew even at that age what the answer would be, and why.

"I'm busy," Red John said briefly. "How's everything at

the ranch? How's Maw's sprained ankle?"

That was the first Tam knew that Red John kept contact with their mother, and he sensed dimly the mother love whose strength defied her stern husband. There in the open road they talked a full half an hour, and then Red John rode on with his men.

Jeremiah Matson died. Their mother followed. The great drought came. Gaunt cattle starved by thousands. Mortgage foreclosures swept the range country like a devouring curse. In those years the fame of Red John Matson still grew. Legends were told about him. Men were shot down around him and bullets cut his clothing. Now and then he was cornered by a posse—and yet somehow Red John always escaped.

All that drifted into the Coffee Pot range, and Tam Matson heard and remembered that night when a big arm hugged him close. Tam was twenty-two when the horse ranch passed into other hands. He wasn't sorry. The three years he had managed the place alone had been increasingly restless years. The dry range and encircling mountains had become barriers hemming him in—the hard times had been increasingly difficult.

Six thousand dollars changed hands in the transaction. Half of it Tam banked in the name of his brother, for Jeremiah Matson, stern and unrelenting to the last, had willed everything to Tam, but to Tam it was fitting that brothers share equally. Then Tam rode off the Coffee Pot range with all he owned on a pack horse.

In the months that followed he sought Red John Matson. From Yuma to the Little Colorado Tam rode, and east across the high mountains to Denver, and down south through the Río Grande valley to El Paso, following the

11

vague, illusive trail of rumor. Men smiled at his requests for news of Red John. This quiet, smiling, blue-eyed young man who waited hopefully for their answers had little in common with Red John Matson, outlaw. He was not an officer trying to make an arrest. He was not an outlaw. And, when they ordered liquor, he asked for water and ignored the laughter it provoked.

In El Paso the trail was warm. A deputy sheriff had recognized Red John and tried to arrest him. Shots had been exchanged. The deputy had fled with one arm shot up, and Red John had crossed the Río Grande into Mexico with four men.

The bearded rancher who told it ordered another drink on Tam Matson. "I reckon Red John'll stay over in Mexico a while," the rancher declared with morbid satisfaction. "It's gettin' too hot north of the line for him. You seem mighty keen about him, young feller. Red John owe you any money?"

Other men chuckled at his humor.

"If he did, I guess he'd pay it," Tam said calmly. "I wonder who'd know where Red John is across the border?"

"Tomás Cortéz in Juárez can tell you, son. He knows everything that happens north of Mexico City."

"And who," Tam asked, "is Tomás Cortéz that he knows so much?"

"Old Cortéz is the devil, an' hell's too cold to hold him," said the bearded rancher, pouring himself another drink. "He ain't the military governor of Chihuahua, but he can tell the governor what to do. He don't own an acre of land, an' yet there's a thousand *haciendas* he can have fer the asking. He ain't never been seen with a gun, but there's plenty Mexicans who'd shove a knife in their throats if Tomás Cortéz told 'em to."

12

Tam drained the water in his glass. His blue eyes were mild, dreamy. "It takes plenty of man to do that," he said. "I hope Cortéz doesn't tell me to put a knife in my throat."

The rancher stared at him. "Hell, kid! You going over to see that old man of Satan?"

"Figured I might."

"You'll learn better when you get older. If you don't come back, I'll spread the word what happened to you."

Tam Matson rode across the old wooden bridge that spanned the muddy Río Grande. His blue eyes were curious as he looked on low, gay-painted adobe houses, on black-shawled Mexican women, and brown-skinned children playing in the hot, white dust. He racked his horses in front of a *cantina* and took his quest to the Mexican bartender inside. A stare, a shrug, a shake of the head was his answer.

"No savvy," said the bartender briefly. He slopped a damp rag on the bar top and mopped busily. "Wheeskey?" he asked.

"Nothing," said Tam.

Outside, a man listened to Tam's question, looked startled, shook his head, and walked on hastily, looking back once over his shoulder. He questioned a score of men without success. No one admitted knowing Tomás Cortéz or where he might be found. Then, through the hot afternoon sunlight, a barefoot Mexican boy came running as Tam was about to swing into the saddle and ride on to the next *cantina*.

"*Señor,*" said the boy, "you weesh *Señor* Cortéz?"

Tam dropped his foot from the stirrup. "You bet I do. Know where he is?"

"No savvy English, *señor.*"

"Savvy Tomás Cortéz?"

13

The boy ducked his head, grinning, and beckoned. "You come." He trotted off through the dust, looking back over his shoulder.

Tam rode after him. The boy led him past the sleepy plaza, past the great looming gray cathedral, and on through narrow dusty streets where stucco house-fronts formed an unbroken line along the walks. At a hitch rack midway of a block of such buildings, the boy stopped. He waited in an open doorway until Tam joined him, and then padded back through a cool, shaded passageway into a sunny patio where tropical flowers rioted in color and a great gaudy macaw screeched from a wooden perch.

On the shaded side of the patio a fat old man with a white mustache sat holding a cold drink in a tall glass and stared unblinkingly as the boy brought Tam to him. He listened to the boy a moment, tossed a coin, waved him away, and then he bluntly said to Tam: "I hear you ask for me, *señor?*"

Tam shifted his gun belt, stood in his scuffed, high-heeled boots looking down at the Mexican. This placid old man could hardly be the one he had been hearing about, he thought. The boy who had brought him here had not been afraid of this one, and there was nothing about the fat old man to breed fear. Then, looking closer, Tam caught the hard, unblinking regard and saw what he had thought fat was solid beef and muscle.

The macaw screeched raucously, sidling along the perch. Tam looked about the patio. They were alone, and yet he had the feeling that eyes were watching them and ears listening.

"You're a hard man to find, *señor,*" he said politely.

The old man's glance became dry, humorous. His English was good, accented only slightly. "Not so hard to find, *señor,*" he said slyly. "Even the *muchachos . . .* the little boys

14

. . . know where Tomás Cortéz sits in the afternoon."

Cortéz sipped his cold drink, leisurely smoothed his fierce white *mustachios,* did not ask Tam to sit down. He waited for Tam to speak.

"I hear you know everything in the north of Mexico," Tam finally said.

Cortéz shrugged. "Old women talk in the market place," he said idly. "*¿Quién sabe? Sí, señor,* who knows anything? What can an old man sunning himself in this patio know about the north of Mexico?"

Cortéz regarded Tam over the glass rim with lazy-lidded indifference, but Tam caught that hard, unblinking regard when he first came in. Behind the half-closed lids now the stare was still appraising him keenly. Tam had seen a score of men lie hastily about knowledge of Tomás Cortéz.

"I'm lookin' for Red John Matson."

For a moment the sharp eyes of Tomás Cortéz stabbed like a rapier. "Why do you come to me?" he asked.

"Because," said Tam patiently, "it is said you know everything in the north of Mexico. John Matson rode into Juárez with four men a week ago. I want him."

"For the law?" Cortéz inquired.

"I'm Red John Matson's brother."

Then Tomás Cortéz made no secret about his look. Easily, despite the bulk of his torso, he sat erect, leaned forward. "The brother of Red John Matson? I have not heard Red John Matson has a brother."

"I reckon you only know everything in the north of Mexico," Tam told him. "I'm Red John's brother."

"So?" said Tomás Cortéz. "And he knows you seek him?"

"I haven't seen him since I was twelve. He's been an outlaw. I've been on the home ranch. I just missed him in

El Paso. I'm following until I find him."

Cortéz twirled his *mustachios*, fished tobacco and brown papers from his pocket, rolled a cigarette deftly, talking as he did so. "You are not an outlaw, then? And you wish to find your brother who is an outlaw?"

"Yes."

Cortéz moistened the paper with the tip of his tongue, shaped the cylinder deftly. "All who travel with Red John Matson become outlaws," he said. "You, too?"

"*¿Quién sabe?*" said Tam without emotion.

"You speak Spanish?"

"*Un poco.*"

Cortéz snapped a match with his thumbnail, inhaled deeply, and the chair creaked as he settled his bulk in it. His eyes were still studying Tam. "My young friend," he said, dribbling smoke up past his eyes, "can you shoot?"

"Good enough."

"That," said Cortéz, "might not be good enough . . . in the north of Mexico." He tossed the rest of his drink on the ground. "I will throw this glass in the air. Can you break it? Are you ready?"

"Wait!" said Tam. "I don't give a damn what you think of my shooting. I came here to get news of Red John Matson. Put your glass down."

"No man who cannot break this glass in the air should look for Red John," Cortéz said. "If you cannot break it, my young friend, I, Tomás Cortéz, can only tell you to ride back across the Río Grande and stay."

"I don't know what you've got on your mind," Tam said slowly, "but pitch that glass up, mister."

Since there must be this play-acting about the matter, Tam waited. Not until the glass left the muscular hand did Tam's palm slap to his gun. He found time to meet the old man's hard, interested stare. Then, as the glass paused for an instant, level with the roof, the patio rang with the shot. The glass dissolved in space, rained down in fragments.

Replacing the gun, Tam said curtly: "If that'll make you talk about Red John, go ahead. I've been doing kid tricks like that since I was old enough to haul back the hammer on a gun."

"Kid tricks?" said Tomás Cortéz softly. He stroked his mustachios, beamed. Reserve vanished in open friendliness. "*Amigo,* you shall go to your brother. I have heard that Red John has gone south to Guadalupe. A man I know goes to Guadalupe, *mañana.* He will guide you."

Tam smiled thinly. "I had an idea it wasn't only the old women who heard things. Why can't we leave now?"

"*Mañana,*" said Cortéz firmly. "At daybreak. Come to this house as the sun rises. The man will be ready. And, my young friend," said Tomás Cortéz unsmilingly, "until you see your brother, do not say that you have seen Tomás Cortéz or that you know Red John Matson!" Cortéz paused. "The silent man lives longest," he finished.

II

That night Tam slept in El Paso where the beds were cleaner and his throat somewhat safer. Then in the chill, gray dawn he rode once more across the river, through silent streets, and came to the hitch rack. A pack horse and saddled mule were tied there. Against the pink stucco wall of Tomás Cortéz's house a man crouched with a serape over an arm, and Tam saw that the man wore a *bandolera* of cartridges over one shoulder and a gun belt at his waist.

17

Thin, short, slow-moving, the stranger untied the pack horse and climbed on the mule.

"I am Pedro," he said in Spanish. "Are you ready, *señor?*"

"*Sí.*"

Together they rode out of Juárez through the chill dawn, south over the great brown plain ahead, while the rising sun spun gold in the eastern sky and drove the chill away. Slowly the white glare of day drowned the world in heat.

Pedro talked little. Once his gun lashed out and the bullet shattered the neck of a sluggish rattler half coiled beside the dusty road. Then with the gun back in the holster, Pedro gave Tam a thin-lipped grin over white teeth.

Tam grinned back and said briefly: "*Bueno.*"

A jack rabbit burst from a clump of mesquite, and Tam dropped it at fifty yards with his belt gun. It was half luck, but Pedro's grin was broader, his teeth flashed whiter.

"*¡Bueno! ¡Bueno!*" he called vigorously. Thereafter he seemed friendlier. Pointing to the mountains on the northwest horizon, he said: "Guadalupe!" He held up five fingers, then two. "Guadalupe!" he repeated, waving his arm at the mountains.

Seven days' ride to Guadalupe. . . .

The fifth day they came down from high, forested slopes into a broad valley cut by a traveled road and the winding loops of a river. All afternoon they followed the valley, passing through small settlements of unplastered adobe huts. That night at sunset they camped on the riverbank.

"*Dos mas días,*" Pedro said.

As Pedro fried two rabbits he had shot that afternoon, Tam squatted by the campfire and thought of Guadalupe, two days ahead. Pedro had told him something of

Guadalupe—a small mining town back in the mountains. There were Guadalupes all over Mexico. Tam had expected a fair-size town. Pedro had said it was a small place where the *norteamericanos* mined gold from the rich Guadalupe vein. The nearest city was Montejo, where General Tamalis represented the military governor of Chihuahua.

Pedro had spat at the name of General Tamalis. Tam had noticed and asked casually: "What's wrong with Tamalis?"

Pedro spat again, pulled up his sleeve, pointed to a great lined scar on his left forearm. Turning the sizzling chunks of rabbit with his knife point, he spoke bitterly of General Santiago Tamalis. Three-quarters Indian, half wolf, half devil, Pedro called the general, said—"Someday . . ."—and stabbed through a chunk of meat so viciously the knife rang on the metal beneath.

Tam came to his feet as a loud voice drifted through the new dark to them. "By God, Jake, it smells good! We'll grub up here!"

Two riders galloped from the road, dismounted, carrying rifles. One of the men swaggered to the fire, cast an appraising eye at the frying pan, addressed Tam loudly.

"Hell, you're an *americano*, ain't you? Thought you was Mexicans. Jake, how does the grub smell?" He was bearded, squat, heavy, his legs were bowed, his voice loud, his manner boisterous. He spat, tilted his sombrero. "My belly's plenty flat. I could eat a mule. How 'bout you, Jake?"

"Sure," Jake said briefly.

Jake was tall, raw-boned, bearded, also. Both men wore two belt guns, had a *bandolera* of cartridges over a shoulder, and carried a repeating carbine. Pedro said nothing, looking from the corners of his eyes as he squatted by the fire.

"I reckon we've got enough grub for all," Tam said. "How about it, Pedro?"

"*Sí,*" Pedro said. He opened a can of beans, produced a stack of cold tortillas he had bought from a Mexican woman that afternoon. The two visitors fell to without ceremony. When they finished, the short, stocky man wiped his hands on worn leather chaps, rolled a cigarette.

"My name's Ben Clyde," he said. "This is Jake Murphy. What's your handle, kid?"

"Matson," Tam said without thinking.

"Matson? I've heard that name before."

"I had a father."

Clyde laughed boisterously, got to his feet. "That's something, ain't it, Jake? We're obliged for the grub, kid. Do the same for you someday. Where you heading?"

"Just riding around," Tam answered, standing with his back to the fire watching them.

Clyde winked broadly. "That's as good as anything. Well, *adiós.* Thanks again fer the grub."

They rode off. Pedro stared after them. His dark eyes were sultry. "Tonight," he stated, "I will not sleep by the campfire."

But nothing happened that night, and the next morning, as they rode off, Tam grinned at Pedro. "If *americanos* make you sleep away from the campfire, you'd better not go north of the border, *amigo.*"

Pedro shrugged. "I have seen coyotes before," he said.

They rode all day until after dark, made camp by a little brawling mountain stream. Before daybreak they were in the saddle again. Under the high, hot sun they came down into a small valley, which drove back farther into the mountains, and up, following the rocky bed of a small stream.

Every hour or so they met long strings of horses carrying ore sacks.

"To Montejo," Pedro said briefly.

"Heap of trouble to carry all that out thisaway, ain't it?" Tam asked.

"*Muy rico* . . . very rich ore," Pedro told him.

Presently they rode around a sharp bend of the road and the thin snaps of two rifle shots sounded ahead. Tam heard the shrill whine of the bullet that tore through the crown of his Stetson.

Pedro lurched in his saddle, kicked his feet free, and tumbled into the dust. Tam made a flying leap for two great boulders on the left bank.

III

Two more shots followed Tam. A bullet kicked up dust on the bank ahead of him. He heard its angry, glancing buzz into space as he reached the shelter of the rocks and flopped down, pumping a shell into the rifle he had carried with him.

Pedro lay where he had fallen, grotesquely spread-eagled in the dust. His mule backed off. The brawling current down in the streambed was the only sound.

Tam held up his hat. Instantly a bullet drilled the crown. A second bullet ricocheted off the rock beside the hat. Only two men were up ahead there, behind a pile of rocks where the road swung to the left out of sight. Propping his hat so that the crown was just visible, Tam crawled to the edge of the boulders, found a crack through which he could see. Slowly he pushed the rifle through, waited patiently.

Sunlight glinted slightly on moving metal ahead. Tam squeezed the trigger. Dust flew beside that metal glint. Both guns bombarded the boulders again, aiming at the hat crown.

Tam swore softly. Tomás Cortéz must have known what he was talking about when he had warned of danger. But this didn't have much sense. He and Pedro did not look like men who might be carrying money.

Pedro rolled suddenly in the dust, scrambled to the boulders, threw himself flat as lead sang past. *"¡Dios!"* he panted in Spanish. "I think I am killed, then! *Carramba,* I should have looked for this!"

"How so?"

"Those two! No one else could have brought word we were coming!"

Looking over his rifle sights, Tam asked thoughtfully: "What difference does it make if we are coming?"

"¡Ai!" exclaimed Pedro. *"¡Mucho!"*

Pedro's shoulder was wet with blood. Gingerly he removed his coat, and slashed his shirt open, revealing a ragged flesh wound. "It's not much," he said. "I think we live, eh, *amigo?*"

"Hope so." Tam was studying the mountain slope beyond them. A small depression ran from the road up the slope and out of sight. It was not more than three or four feet deep.

In Spanish Tam said: "I'll get them."

"Sí," Pedro agreed wryly. "But how?"

"Watch me."

Tam lifted his head, ducked down again instantly. The brief exposure drew two quick shots. An instant later Tam sprinted for the depression, made it, dropped down out of sight as bullets sang harmlessly over his head.

On hands and knees he crawled up that shallow depression to a little shelf, studded with cacti and small bushes. Screened by small trees, he advanced cautiously. Minutes later he heard the pound of hoofs receding along the road. Plunging down to the shelf, he was just in time to see two riders disappearing around a bend in the road.

In the distance one rider looked short, thick-set, the other tall, lanky. The rock pile ambush was deserted when he got to it.

Joining Pedro, he said: "You were right. It was those two we fed."

"*Si,*" said Pedro, nodding.

More than once in the hours that followed Tam wished for that rough, winding road along the streambank instead of this mountain road over which Pedro led him. Pedro's big mule, climbing like a mountain goat, threaded up through the trees on dizzying slopes.

The sun dropped out of sight over the high mountain crest. Daylight slowly gathered the night chill, and still Pedro led the way higher, angling at times along the slopes until he found an easier way. They finally topped a high, forested ridge and rode down the other side. Darkness was falling when Pedro turned up a narrow little cañon, struck a faint trail, and said with satisfaction: "Now we will come to Guadalupe from the back."

Darkness had been about them for two full hours when lights appeared ahead. They heard a man's voice raised in song in the far distance. Then the intermittent sounds of mining machinery, and the trees gave way to barren slopes that had been denuded of timber. They rode into a mile-wide flat cradled on three sides by still higher slopes.

Against the base of the hill ahead they could see lights

about the opening of the mine. Below the mine Guadalupe huddled in a blot of low buildings under the faint light of a half moon riding high in the sky.

Pedro heaved a sigh of relief, crossed himself in the moonlight. "Thanks to God we arrive," he said. "What is it we find, *amigo?*"

"Who knows?" said Tam.

But they made it. The peace of the encircling peaks lay over Guadalupe as they rode slowly between the outlying houses. Doors were shut, windows closed; where there was light, it was curtained. Dogs barked—there were always dogs, Tam had found, in these Mexican towns—but there was no one abroad in the streets. A brooding hush gripped Guadalupe—not the hush of sleep nor the exhaustion of hard labor, but the hush of tense waiting.

"This I do not understand," Pedro said, puzzled. "Guadalupe does not sleep so. The *cantinas* never close. There are men . . . *carramba,* and women, if one wishes . . . in the streets until sunrise. There is music and laughter and talk. *¡Dios!* Have I not seen it many times? And now . . . Guadalupe is dead." Pedro loosened his belt and felt his gun in the holster.

But, as they penetrated deeper among the houses, nothing happened. Once Tam thought he saw a walking figure give one startled look in their direction and dodge out of sight. He rode on to that point with his hand near his gun. But the man was gone.

Then, abruptly, they were in the plaza, and the mine lights were visible on the mountain slope beyond. In the plaza were trees and benches. A small group of men under the nearest trees turned and stared as the two rode up. The men drew close together, as cattle bunch in the face of danger. Pedro addressed them.

24

"Buenas noches, amigos."

A man or two mumbled an answer. They seemed easier after seeing that Pedro was Mexican.

"Where are the people?" Pedro asked them.

No one answered.

"Are you without tongues?" Pedro demanded angrily. "Where is the *yanqui* with the red hair?"

One man answered that. "In the *cantina* of the Green Parrot," he said.

"Gracias," Pedro grunted.

The *cantina* had the brightest windows on the plaza and the only sign of life and merriment. Horses stood at the hitch rack. Through open doors came guitar music and loud singing. Through the windows, as they rode up and dismounted, Tam saw men. At least a dozen horses were tied at the hitch rack.

Pedro took his rifle from the saddle scabbard. Tam did the same, although he was no longer uneasy. If Red John were inside, everything was all right.

Pedro stepped through the doorway and swept the room inside with a glance. Tam did the same. The dozen men were strung along the bar and scattered about the room. Several were dancing with Mexican girls. At the back of the room three natives were strumming guitars and singing. As the strangers entered, the dancers stopped. Men turned, stared at them.

Standing at the far end of the bar was a big, broad-shouldered man whose bare head was topped by a flaming shock of red hair. Tam ignored the rest of the company as he walked the length of the room. They faced each other, the older, heavier man and the younger, slimmer one.

Tam met a wooden stare with a grin and said: "Hello,

Johnny." Inside, he felt warm and at peace. He knew he was not mistaken. This was Red John, wearing a plain cowhide vest with the hair out and sky-blue Army trousers whose yellow cavalry stripe ran down into old, worn boots.

A gathering scowl met his grin. Red John's left hand had been toying with an empty whiskey glass. His fingers slowly revolved the glass.

"What's the idea of callin' me Johnny?" he asked roughly.

"It came kinda natural, I guess. I'm Tam, your brother. I guess you remember me."

The guitars had stopped playing. Every eye in the room was looking at them; every ear was listening to what they said. Red John stood there and looked Tam up and down. The scowl remained. Tam wasn't sure he heard right when Red John snapped: "You must have a skin full of hooch, young fella. I haven't got a brother. Never did have a brother. Get outta here an' ride on. You're scratchin' me the wrong way."

IV

Tam stopped smiling. The warm glow vanished. The words were plain enough, but they didn't make sense.

"You're Red John Matson, aren't you?" he questioned uncertainly.

"Hell, yes . . . if it's any of your business. Now beat it. Get outta here. Don't you savvy English? Do I have to throw you out?"

Tam rubbed the side of his chin with his palm. He was bewildered and didn't care if it showed. He had looked for anything but this. His mouth hardened a little, and his voice, too.

"I've been lookin' for you for months," he said. "Dad died, an' I sold out and banked your share an' came looking for you. It took me a long time to catch up."

Red John put the empty whiskey glass on the bar. His scowl deepened. "You've got the wrong man. Get out! Savvy?" Red John drew his gun and jammed it into Tam's stomach.

Tam saw it coming. He could have drawn his own gun. But he only stood there, and beneath the hard muzzle shoving into his middle a cold, sick feeling grew. He searched Red John's face and found no softness there.

Tam nodded. "I reckon you're right," he agreed bitterly. "I haven't got a brother. I reckon I never did have one. I've been a damned fool. Put up your gun, mister. I'm going."

Something flickered in Red John's eyes. It looked like pain. Red John holstered his gun and spoke indifferently. "Go to the mine office an' tell 'em your story. Maybe they'll know who you're lookin' for."

Along the bar a man laughed, and swaggered out on the floor and faced them, speaking with a sneer. "That's a pretty little act you're puttin' on, Red. But it ain't worth a damn. So you got a brother, huh? Hell, I knew this mornin' the kid was headin' this way to you. But I didn't figure he was your brother."

The speaker stood half a head taller than Red John himself. He must have weighed fifty pounds more. He wore two guns and rawhide chaps studded with silver *conchas*. Big rowelled spurs jingled as he stepped. A black curly beard covered the lower part of his face and a gray sombrero tilted forward over the upper part.

Red John hunched his shoulders, put his back against

the bar. The hardness of his voice grew cold. "You know a lot, Bull. Fact is, I never knew when Bull Snyder didn't think he knew every damn' thing there was to know. But this ain't any of your business. I'm invitin' you to step back and keep on with your drinkin'."

White teeth showed through the curly beard as Bull Snyder laughed. "You're invitin' *me?* Hell, I'm *tellin'* you, Red. Did you think we come here to drink?"

"I figured that was all you'd like to do, Bull."

Several men along the bar edged nearer to Red John. They were dressed as Red John was, in old clothes, showing the marks of hard use. Each man had a rifle in his hand. Then, beyond them, Tam saw the two men Pedro and he had fed, the two men who had tried to bushwhack them down the cañon road. Ben Clyde, the loud-mouthed one, was grinning at him. The tall, saturnine Jake Murphy stood there watching. As light breaks through fog, Tam saw that the men in this crude *cantina* room were in two parties, and edging apart.

The girls who had been dancing with the men were moving toward a door at the back of the room. Sharp, growing tension was filling the air.

Bull Snyder spat on the floor. "We rode into town lookin' for you, Red. An' since we walked in here, we been watchin' you an' these maverick runners of yours wiggle an' squirm an' try to figger what to do."

"I reckon we know what to do, Bull." From the corner of his mouth, Red John said: "Kid, get out that back door."

"Let him stay," Bull Snyder sneered. "We'll take the pup with the old dog. Or maybe you'd rather climb on your hosses an' head back over the border."

Red John's elbows were back on the bar. His voice grew more casual. "Figurin' we're only five against eight of you,

28

Bull? Seems to me that's about the odds you always like. Where'd you pick up these extra calf butchers you brought along?"

Abruptly Snyder grew ugly. "Meanin' what?"

"Meanin' you're a low-down, yellow, double-crossin' skunk who'd cut his grandmother's throat if she had a Mex' *peso* he wanted," said Red John casually. "If there's anybody ridin' back across the border, it'll be you, Bull. Play your hand."

Pedro's soft hiss of warning jerked Tam's head around toward the back of the room. A man with a leveled rifle had stepped noiselessly into that back doorway. At the same moment that Bull Snyder yelled—"All right, boys!"—his hand came up with a gun.

In the back room a girl screamed. Pedro sprang out from the bar. But Tam saw only that man standing there with his rifle aimed at Red John. With the woman's scream ringing in his ears, Tam drew his gun, drew it with the smooth speed years of practice had perfected. This was the first time he had ever drawn like this to kill, but he was cool, surprisingly cool, and he had never shot quicker.

But he couldn't outshoot a man whose finger already was on the trigger. The bark of the rifle shot came a breath before his own gun spoke. Behind him he heard Red John's gun go off and the roar of a gun where Bill Snyder was standing.

The leveled rifle in the doorway dropped down. The man who held it wobbled queerly as his knees buckled and his head jerked grotesquely to one side. Tam saw the little dark hole open in the cheek, just above the jaw, and noted mechanically that his bullet had hit a little low and to one side. But the stranger would fire no more rifle bullets.

Whirling, Tam saw Bull leaping backward across the

room, and men scattering out beyond him. Red John, with his back still against the bar, was fanning his gun. Bull Snyder was not shooting now. He had no gun. His hand was spurting blood.

A bullet splintered the bar edge beside Tam. He saw a man across the room swing a gun muzzle toward Red John. Tam shot. The man staggered, dodged aside, shifting his gun to the other hand. His arm was crippled.

Then Bull Snyder caught up a chair and hurled it at the lamp. The room went dark. Three scattered gun flashes laced the blackness like angry, vicious tongues.

Bull Snyder's bellow rose above all other sounds. "Outside, boys!"

Tam emptied his gun toward the sound. A bullet went through his hat, another seared his shoulder as more guns flashed. Then, as suddenly as it had started, the gunfire stopped.

Feet scuffled at the front door. Men swore there. Horses snorted and stamped at the hitch rack. Red John's voice grated from the bar. "Run 'em out of town, boys! Keep 'em a-going!"

Forgetting all that had passed between them, Tam wheeled when Red John's voice broke into a half gasp. "You all right, Johnny?" he asked.

Red John answered gruffly. "You still here? Sure I'm all right. Shut up an' keep quiet!"

But Tam was already running toward the door, reloading as he went. Outside he found confusion. Men were riding away from the hitch rack and stringing out along the plaza. One of Red John's men wheeled his horse away from the hitch rack, emptying his gun after the retreating riders as he followed them. Tam was in the saddle behind him a moment later, leaving behind a storm of Spanish oaths as

Pedro fought a bucking horse.

Riding hard, gun out and ready, Tam felt an exaltation he had never before known. Death had faced him back there in the *cantina* and he had not been afraid. Death fled there ahead of him and he felt no fear in following.

Gunfire hammered in the night ahead. Snyder and his men were riding out of the plaza, shooting as they went at the dark scurrying forms of the Mexicans who Pedro had questioned.

In the dim moonlight Tam saw a dark figure lying in the dust, then another off to the right, flopping queerly and crying out in pain. Just beyond the wounded men, the door of a low adobe house opened and a woman came out.

For an instant Tam saw her against the faint yellow lamplight from the doorway. He saw the light on blonde hair and white skin, and in mid-stride wheeled his horse to the wounded man and the woman. She was no native, such as belonged in a mean little house like that. She was white, she looked American, and she had no business out here in the open night.

She was kneeling by the wounded man when Tam reined in beside them. He had been right about her. Without rising she looked up. Her bitter words rose above the groans of the wounded man.

"Get away! You've done enough!"

From the saddle Tam warned her. "Get back in that house, ma'am. You've got no business out here . . . now."

"He's dying!" she wrenched out. She was sobbing and had no fear of him. "He was unarmed, trying to get into his house, and your men shot him down as if he were a dog! Get out before I kill you, too!" she cried fiercely.

She had been carrying a gun which Tam had not seen until it swung up at him now. He reined over hard and ducked—and she shot up at him.

How close she came he never knew. The report and flash under his horse's nose sent that sorely tried animal bolting and bucking away from the spot. He came to the edge of the plaza before he got the animal under control.

The gunshots had died away at the edge of town. The girl evidently could take care of herself. Tam left her there in the plaza and rode through dark, narrow streets toward the mine lights.

On the sloping mountainside enough land had been leveled for the shaft head and hosting machinery. Above, below, and on both sides the low adobe buildings clustered, as if built there to hem in and protect the mine itself. The lights Tam had seen in the distance were from windows and big outside lanterns. In front of the nearest and longest building four men were standing with rifles ready. Four Americans, Tam saw as he rode to them, and the rifles covered him as he came.

"Where'd Red John Matson an' his men go?" Tam called to them.

They waited, staring at him, until he was close, and then the tallest man snapped: "Who the devil are you?"

They had no friendliness for him. Tam remembered suddenly that Red John and his men were outlaws, and he wondered which of the four rifles might shoot first. But he had to account for himself now.

"I'm with Red John Matson," he told them.

A second man, younger than the first, snapped from under a black mustache: "You're a liar! We know Matson and his men!"

"I just got in."

"From where?"

"Juárez," Tam said, and cocked his head and listened to

a horse coming through the darkness along the hill slope. It was walking, and only the silence that had fallen over the spot made the *click* of hoofs against small stones audible. The mine men heard it, also. Two of them faced that way with their rifles ready, while the younger man demanded harshly: "Who are you?"

"Nobody sent me, mister. I came lookin' for Red John. I heard he was here."

But the other insisted: "Who told you Matson was here?"

Since one way seemed equally as dangerous as another now, Tam told the truth. "A man named Cortéz told me Red John'd be here at Guadalupe. An' if you'll pull those rifles off me, I'll feel better. Red John is all I want. If he went past here, I'll ride on an' look for him."

The tall first speaker demanded sharply: "Cortéz sent you?"

"That's right, mister."

"Why didn't you say so? Matson's men rode along the mountain there. Who is this coming? Isn't that Matson?"

It was! Red John rode alone, on a slow-walking horse, sagging forward, holding on with both hands to keep from falling from the saddle.

V

Tam was at Red John's side a moment later. "What is it, Johnny?" he asked, reining around. With a visible effort Red John straightened in the saddle. In lantern light his face looked gray and drawn, and, when he spoke, his voice was thick and labored. But he managed to smile.

"You all right, kid?" Red John asked.

"Sure. But Johnny, you're hit, ain't you?"

"Kinda," Red John replied. "I was afraid they'd get you back there in the saloon. Tried to run you off, an' Snyder called my hand. You damn', stubborn young fool, what'd you mean comin' south of the border into this patch of hell? I oughta. . . ."

Red John swayed in the saddle. He would have fallen if Tam hadn't leaned over and steadied him.

The mining men were about them now. "Get him outta the saddle. He's hit bad," Tam said huskily.

Two of the men were already reaching to do that. Tam helped them carry Red John into the long building, which was the mine office, and back into a rear room to a cot.

Through the open front of his vest, Red John's shirt front was blotched with smears of fresh blood. Halfway up his left leg the yellow cavalry stripe of his stained trousers was colored red with more blood.

Red John was conscious, but weak, very weak. Two of the younger men began to get off his clothes. The third opened a medical kit on a table, and Red John grinned up at the tall man who had given orders.

"Looks like I'm throwed an' hobbled for a little, Mister Gray. Snyder busted loose down there finally. We made it a little hotter than he figured, so he vamoosed back into the hills. Three, four of his men are down there in the Green Parrot. They'll be good for a while. Meet my kid brother."

Gray looked startled. "Your brother?"

Red John swallowed painfully. His face was getting grayer, but the smile stayed there. "He's as good a man as I am. Cortéz sent him with a Mexican. Tam, I reckon you know this is Alexander Gray, the owner of the Guadalupe."

From Alexander Gray Tam got one of the sharpest looks

he had ever received. He was a tall, spare man, in leather leggings and canvas trousers and coat. Alexander Gray's black hair was turning white at the temples and a close-cropped mustache was grizzled, too.

"So Tomás Cortéz sent you?" Gray said. "Did you bring any message?"

"Nope. Maybe Pedro did. He came from Cortéz."

"Where is he?"

"He followed Snyder's men."

Alexander Gray looked disturbed. "He must have had some message. I hope he doesn't get killed before he delivers it. Matson, how many men have you now?"

"Can't say," Red John replied weakly. "Couple went down in the fracas. I didn't stay to see if they stayed down. They're tough *hombres*. I reckon we can count Cortéz's Mexican, an' Tam here, an' maybe a couple more . . . say four. It'll be another week before any more get here."

The man with the medical instruments had rolled up his sleeves and washed his hands while they talked. He stepped to Red John and began a quick examination. Slender, professional-looking, he spoke with clipped words as he worked.

"I should have your daughter here, Mister Gray."

"Step over to the house and get her, Healy," Alexander Gray requested.

A tall, awkward-looking man, Healy left the room with shambling movements surprisingly fast. But he had hardly gotten out the front door when a horse galloped up.

Healy's startled voice was audible. "Good Lord, Miss Gray! You haven't been down in town, have you?"

She answered breathlessly as she came in the front door. "I walked down to see a sick woman for a few minutes. And they killed her husband in front of the house! The beasts shot him down like an animal! And there are three wounded men and dead men in the Green Parrot! I took one of their horses and came here to get Doctor Murphy."

She hurried into the front room—and Tam faced again the woman who had shot at him in the plaza. He saw now that she was a girl younger than he, and in the light her hair was more yellow than at his first glimpse. She was slender and quick, and in one hand she carried a revolver. The sleeve of her jacket and the side of her skirt were stained with blood.

Her small, oval face hardened as she recognized Tam. "Did you catch this one, Dad?" she asked Alexander Gray hastily.

"That is Matson's brother, Lia. Doctor Murphy needs you. Matson is badly wounded. The other wounded men will have to wait."

The light was turned low. Alexander Gray walked the floor slowly, smoking a cigarette, talking nervously. Lia Gray sat by the cot, and Red John lay under blankets when the doctor finished with him, pale, quiet, eyes open as he listened.

"Another incident like this and all the workers will be gone," Gray said heavily. "I can't blame them. They know something is wrong. They can see that they're not getting protection. What do you think Snyder is going to do next, Matson?"

Red John's voice was weak but clear. "Show up with more men. He wouldn't 'a' pulled his freight so fast, if he didn't have an ace comin' up in the deck. I put a hole through his arm, but that didn't take the orneriness outta him."

Lia Gray sat up straight and spoke angrily. "If I were in

36

Mexico City, I could do something about this. You know how close I was to the president's daughter in school, Dad."

"I've told you to forget that," Alexander Gray remarked to his daughter with finality. "Mexico City won't interfere in a small matter like this. They've enough trouble at present. Tamalis is running these parts and taking his orders from Chihuahua."

"He's right," Red John said from the cot. "Tamalis is backed from Chihuahua. An' old General Cordova in Chihuahua is pretty sure how he stands or he wouldn't be backing it."

"What's it all about?" Tam asked from the foot of the cot. "In Juárez, Cortéz hinted there'd be plenty of trouble after I got here, but he didn't let on what it was."

Alexander Gray had resumed his pacing. Without stopping, he spoke soberly. "Several years ago I purchased rights to this mine from Tomás Cortéz. It was a profitable deal for both of us. At that time Cortéz's word was practically law in Chihuahua. Since then a strong military governor, Tamalis, has practically taken over the state. He's trying to break Cortéz by undermining him indirectly. He's decided to get this mine. It would be a small fortune at no cost. In addition, it would prove that Cortéz was losing his grip.

"Tamalis, who heads the garrison of Montejo, where all the ore for this district is smelted, is worse than Cordova at Chihuahua City. The simplest way would be for soldiers to run us out. But that's too open. It would probably make trouble between Washington and Mexico City.

"So Tamalis found a better way. He's letting a band of Yankee outlaws from north of the border do the trick by terrorizing our workers. Washington can't very well protest against actions of its own citizens. All Tamalis has to do is to give help by withholding protection, which he is doing. I've appealed to Tomás Cortéz"—Alexander Gray lit a fresh cigarette—"and he sent back word that he would do what he could. In the meantime, he told me to fight fire with fire, and he sent Matson here with four men to deal with Snyder and his outlaws. Tamalis can't very well take action against them without doing something about Snyder, also. Snyder has more men coming. So has Matson here, but they aren't coming quickly enough."

Alexander Gray's voice hardened into bitterness as he told the story. "Our ore wagons and burro trains going down to the smelter have been stopped time after time. A third of our workers have left Guadalupe already. We'll have to close up the mine shortly if these things keep on going. If Snyder's men destroy the shaft head and the buildings around it, I'm afraid we're through here for good. I was in hopes Matson and his men could protect us for a time. It looks now as if they're not going to be able to."

"You've got men here at the mine," Tam said. "Americans."

"They can't leave the mine," Alexander Gray said curtly. "They're needed here to keep the mine running, and, if Tamalis finds they're fighting in this district, he'll have an excuse to order them away. He told me so. As long as it's outlaw against outlaw, Tamalis shrugs and says he'll do what he can *mañana* . . . which means never, in this case."

Then Lia Gray broke in again. "If you'd only let me go to Mexico City, Dad." Her eyes were bright with anticipation and eagerness. She caught her lower lip between white teeth and looked at Tam. "If I were a man, I'd do something about it!" she said with spirit.

38

Tam smiled at her. "I'll bet you would, miss."

"You *bet* I would."

"The night shift will be leaving the mine as soon as word of this spreads down below," the girl's father broke in. "There's nothing much we can do tonight but keep watch and be ready if Snyder comes back. Lia, you go to bed up at the house. You'll be safe enough there."

Lia Gray started to say something, then nodded obediently and stood up. "Good night," she said, and walked out.

Tam watched admiringly as the door closed behind her. No girl like this had ever crossed his path. Pretty, of course, well-bred, evidently well-educated, she had escaped being soft. Rebellious against inaction, without fear, she seemed a part of this isolated place. He was thinking about how she had run out to the dying man in the plaza when Alexander Gray spoke again.

"As soon as we get the wounded up here, Matson, your men had better get some sleep. My assistants can keep watch tonight."

"I'll stay up," Tam said.

"Get some sleep while you can, kid." Red John settled that. "No telling when you'll need all you got. Bunk over there on the floor. Gray'll give you some blankets."

Dr. Murphy returned. Natives from town brought the two wounded men up and put them on cots in the front office. Tam unsaddled the horses, rubbed them down, left them for the night in the mine stable a little farther up the hill. Then he carried his bedroll in and spread it in one corner of the room where Red John lay.

There, with the lamp turned low and Dr. Murphy occasionally looking in at his patient, Tam slept without dreams. Late that night Pedro rode in, fatigued from his unsuccessful pursuit. He carried no message for Alexander Gray from Tomás Cortéz except to offer his own help.

VI

Sunlight was streaming in the window above Tam when he became aware of a harsh voice speaking. Alexander Gray was standing by Red John's cot.

"She left before midnight!" Gray was saying loudly. "The fool at the stable let her have two horses! I found this note pinned on her pillow!"

Tam was on his feet as Red John asked Alexander Gray if the girl had gone alone, and the mining man answered the bandit. "She took Benedicto Barboa, the man who always rides out with her. He's one of my best men. I don't know what cock-and-bull story she told him. But she's gone"— Alexander Gray choked—"gone to Montejo and on to Mexico City. She's convinced that she can straighten this out through the president's daughter who was her best friend at boarding school."

Red John lay there on the cot, silent for a moment. Then he drawled: "Maybe she can. I've seen some funnier things happen."

"Nonsense, Matson! She . . . she. . . ." Alexander Gray's voice broke. He had to pause a moment before he proceeded. "She's taken her revolver and the two best horses. I'm following her, of course."

"What about the mine?"

"Damn the mine!" said Alexander Gray violently.

Red John lifted a whiskey bottle of water from the floor beside the cot and drank. "You're needed here," he reminded as he put it down.

Gray swung on him. "My daughter's in danger, Matson. I'm going after her!"

Red John stared without expression. "I reckon you'll go," he agreed. "Bull Snyder'll sure like it, too. No use telling you there's a heap of folks around the mine here who need you. Soon as you leave, things'll tangle in a mess. Couple days ago you were sayin' you didn't dare ride off for a half day because the natives'd think you'd been chased away."

They parted on that, but as Gray went out into the chill morning, Tam's throat was tight. Red John had had a fifty-fifty chance the night before. He didn't look that good now.

After a hasty breakfast, Tam and Pedro rode swiftly through Guadalupe where the wood smoke from early fires hung low, and in the sunlight they found it hard to believe that death had stalked among these huddled adobe houses short hours before. The few natives they passed stared dumbly, apathetically. One old crone, somber in a black rebozo, drew a finger across her throat graphically and shrilled unintelligible words after Tam.

"What's she saying?" he called to Pedro.

"She says the devil will drink your blood for the grandson she lost last night."

"Maybe she'll get it. This Bull Snyder and his men are apt to be ahead somewhere."

Pedro shrugged.

"If they caught Miss Gray, I don't reckon they'd hurt her," Tam said.

Pedro shrugged again. "If they are like General Tamalis at Montejo. . . ." He broke off and spat to one side, as he had done before at mention of the man.

"Tamalis wouldn't hurt her. Hell! She's an American!"

41

"All wine looks good to a drunkard," Pedro replied cynically.

"So that's how it is," Tam said. "I guess we'd better get along then."

The long, winding cañon road was deserted. The echoes of their passing drifted up between the steep side slopes, smothered at times by the brawling stream beside the trail. Two shod horses had gone this way ahead of them.

An hour and a half later they met three big ore wagons coming up empty behind long mule teams. Pedro stopped, questioned the men in charge. What Tam didn't understand of the rapid exchange, Pedro made clear as they rode on.

Before daybreak those men had heard riders heading down toward Montejo. From their camp beside the road they had not seen who it was. In Montejo, General Tamalis had been drinking for three days. With his own two hands he had shot two men who had startled the horse he had been riding.

"I reckon," Tam said grimly then, "that we ain't riding hard enough."

From that point on he spared horseflesh no more. The long grade down out of the mountains helped some. But for the first time in his life Tam rode a horse to destruction and put the thought from his mind.

Down, down, hour after hour, with the cañon gradually widening, the slopes on either side becoming less steep. Presently the little river did not run so fast. Patches of flat land appeared, then an occasional adobe hut at the edge of a small field.

Foam flecked both horses. Red flaring nostrils, hard breathing, slackening in the driving stride, warned that flesh and bone could not much longer keep that driving pace.

The slopes became less barren. Presently they were riding past occasional tall stems of the great cacti and on down past increasing mesquite. The cañon abruptly debauched into sandy, rolling foothills covered with more cacti and mesquite, and Montejo lay there ahead of them with the black smelter smoke drifting across the clear blue sky. Buildings crowded the hill slopes along the river. On the highest rise of land the grim, gray walls of an old stone fort overlooked the town.

Pedro walked his spent horse, wiped dust from his face, rolled a cigarette. The sun, at which he cocked an eye, was low against the western line of mountains. To the right, across the sand hills on another road, a long string of ore wagons crawled toward the smelter.

"*Dios*, we are here," Pedro said. "One train in the morning and one train at night, to Torreón, and south, to Mexico City. If she could not make the morning train, we will find her."

The sun dropped from sight, and long purple shadows reached out over Montejo and the evening chill struck through the dry air.

Abruptly, standing in the stirrups, Tam said: "What's that? Looks like soldiers riding this way."

Pedro looked, nodded, said briefly: "*Sí. Soldados.*" He hesitated, then reined his horse off the road toward the nearest sheltering mesquite.

The movement needed no explanation. Tam was following when scattered shots burst from the group of riders. A lone horseman was spurring off to the right toward the nearest sheltering growth, lying low across the horse's neck as he slashed hard with the rein ends. He reeled in the saddle; his horse swerved and came more directly toward them. The men behind spread out fanwise and shot at their leisure.

Even at that distance their deliberate certainty was plain. The horse was limping badly now, hard hit. The rider was swaying in the saddle. Escape was not for him. A stray bullet whined overhead. Pedro, ignoring it, was tense in the saddle as he peered toward the fugitive. His exclamation rose above the sharp snapping of the rifle shots. "*¡Madre de Dios!* Last night in the stable at Guadalupe I saw that horse! Black on one leg, white on the other. See! They kill the man who rode with *Señorita* Gray!"

The purple shadows made a purple shroud for the dying man as Tam galloped down into a dip and up the other slope to the mesquite-dotted level. Pedro raced behind him.

Tam knew they couldn't save the man. Their jaded horses couldn't outrun those fresh mounts of the military. But this man, this Benedicto Barboa who had ridden off to Montejo with Lia Gray, must talk before he died, must tell them what had happened.

Intent on their quarry the soldiers had not seen Tam and Pedro or, if they had, ignored them. Tam was on the level, within a hundred yards of the fugitive, before a distant yell drew attention to him.

Barboa's horse was stumbling now, beginning to weave from side to side in that drunken stagger before the final fall. The rider was holding on with both hands. He was bare-headed, riding sightlessly with his head slumped forward. He did not try to throw himself clear as the horse went down. Limply he went down, too, in the saddle, and would have been crushed had not chance thrown him clear. The horse rolled on the ground, tried to rise, fell back. The man crawled up to one knee and was still trying to rise when Tam hit the ground beside him, demanding: "Are you Barboa?"

The man nodded.

"Where is *Señorita* Gray?"

Barboa was bleeding from chest and shoulder. His eyes were dull, blank as he looked up. And beyond—not far beyond—the fan of soldiers was converging fast on the spot.

Holding the reins with one hand, Tam bent over Barboa. "Miss Gray! The *Señorita* Gray! Where is she? We're from Guadalupe!"

The name got through to Barboa. He was choking now on the blood welling up into his throat. But he managed to lift a hand toward the gray stone fort above the town. He spat blood from his mouth and gasped one word.

"Cortéz!" Barboa gasped, and went down to the ground as if he had clung to life only to speak that one word.

Tam left him there. Bullets were zipping around the spot. The rolling drum of running horses vibrated in a swiftly increasing tide of sound as Tam swung into the saddle.

Pedro spurred off ahead toward the thickest of the mesquite. For a few minutes it looked as if they, too, were doomed. Bullets whined and screamed about them, snapping through the mesquite like vicious insects.

Neither fired back. Perhaps that saved them. For abruptly the shots ceased and the soldiers turned back while Tam and Pedro rode slower, walked their horses, finally stopping.

Pedro drew a deep breath. "In so little more, we, too, would have stayed on the ground."

"Barboa didn't have a chance to escape," Tam mused. "He should 'a' had better sense than to try it."

Pedro's smile in the gathering darkness was sarcastic. "It was not an escape. It was an order to ride on alone," he said. "Barboa knew it was death. When a man is dead, who is to say he was told to ride on alone? Who is to say the bullet in his back killed an innocent man, or one who broke away by force? The men who killed him? No, my friend, not the men who killed him!"

"You mean they brought him out there in the open and told him to ride on, and shot him when he did?"

"*Sí*," said Pedro calmly. "So much simpler than a death by order, about which questions might be asked. A prisoner tries to escape. He must be stopped . . . and, if he dies, the law is plain. It is allowed."

"But Barboa knew. He did not ride down the road so slowly while he waited for those bullets in his back. No! He died hard, riding for the mesquite and the chance his prayers would turn those bullets."

"Perhaps," said Pedro reflectively as he lighted another cigarette, "Barboa did not pray hard enough, or soon enough."

Tam lighted a cigarette, also. He felt cold, colder than the night chill around them, and his voice was troubled.

"We got here too late. Something's happened to Miss Gray," he said.

"*Sí*," Pedro agreed.

"She never got the morning train . . . and she won't get the night train."

"*Sí.*"

"That must mean your friend Tamalis. His orders would have sent those soldiers out after Barboa. An' if Tamalis wanted Barboa dead, you can bet he's up to plenty of dirt."

"*Sí*," Pedro agreed, and it was almost a sigh. Pedro spat and bitter hate was like a file in his voice. "Tamalis would do anything."

They cut across the open rolling hills, struck another road, followed it leisurely in past the first houses and down

46

into Montejo. No one stopped them or questioned them. The unplastered adobe huts gave way to white, gray, pink, and yellow stucco fronts that crowded close to the cobblestone streets over which they presently rode.

Pedro answered his questions with disjointed sentences about the early Spanish *conquistadores* who hundreds of years before had opened the first silver mines in the mountains nearby. Men had burrowed and fought over those silver and gold lodes ever since, while Montejo clung here to the banks of the restless river. The stone fort there on the hilltop had always been there. Now they were coming to the station just ahead, where the railroad started, and would Tam be pleased to stay behind? "A gringo would be no help just now," Pedro said bluntly.

So in the first darkness Tam waited in the saddle beside an old wall while Pedro vanished into the night. Presently Pedro was back, whistling softly between his teeth.

"Come," he said. "Today Tomás Cortéz arrived by train and was met by *Señor* Rafael del Pilary Ruiz, formerly *jefe politico* and a *muy rico caballero* . . . a very rich gentleman."

The house of *Señor* Ruiz was straight ahead at the foot of the hill on which the fortress stood, added Pedro, and doubtless everything would be all right as soon as they talked to *el señor* Cortéz.

Pedro was in better spirits as he wheeled his horse before the iron-studded doors of a long stone house the windows over which the thick curtains were not drawn tightly and so glinted with light. Pedro got down, struck a match, hammered with the massive iron door knocker he located. The street was dark, quiet. The clangor of the knocker echoed loudly. But there was no reply, not even when Pedro knocked again and again. He swore under his breath and tried once more—and, as the sounds died away, men closed in without warning from both ends of the street.

The night was suddenly clamorous with cries, shouted orders. Tam found himself backed against the wall, striking with both fists, driving men back, hurling them away, trying to duck aside and running into still more men. He could have drawn his gun, but Pedro was not shooting. Dead men and doubtful escape would be of no help to Lia Gray. So Tam fought. All around him men panted, swore, crowded in, jamming him back against the rough stone wall. Blows reached him in a dozen places. His lip was cut, cheek split. Dizzy, staggering, he was half blinded as a handful of matches flared suddenly in front of him. Tam never did see the blow that caught him on the head and dropped him.

VII

Pedro was swearing in Spanish heartily, fluently. "Thy father was a burro and thy grandfather was a pig, and, as for the sisters and the grandmothers, if their snouts are so like a pig also, doubtless they. . . ."

Furious curses cut off the rest. Tam opened his eyes and saw the ghastly, unreal flickering of torches beyond thick iron bars. Under the wavering flames men were grinning. A thick-set, bulbous-nosed person in a gold-braided uniform was dancing before the bars and assuring Pedro he would be hanged like a dog before daylight.

The cursing stopped as Tam sat up. He saw that he was in a cell—a dirty, damp, fetid cell, with bare greasy stones for a floor and three walls. Only the fourth side was open, and beyond the bars seven nondescript soldiers were standing behind the officer.

Pedro helped Tam stand up. His comment was philosophical. "The butcher has us," Pedro declared calmly. "It is the will of God."

There was no need to ask who the "butcher" was. This cell could only exist under the old stone fort.

"Is that Tamalis?" Tam asked, nodding at the officer outside the bars, who had swung on his men with an order and was now turning back.

Pedro spat. "That pig is but part of the mud in which Tamalis wallows! He has been waiting for you to recover consciousness. I think we will hang now."

Two soldiers entered the cell with rifles ready.

"They do not know that men can die quietly," Pedro said, staring at Tam. "Come, *amigo.*" Pedro's left eye flashed a quick wink.

They went together, the soldiers surrounding them, the officer strutting behind. Along the passage, through a massive door, to the left along another passage, up stone stairs, more stone stairs, across a courtyard within the fort into a wide, high-ceilinged room where a huge fire crackled and roared in a wide stone fireplace.

The thick, squat man who stepped from the fire to meet them was dressed in a plain black suit. Under the coat a revolver was visible. His mustache was black and curling, his black hair carefully combed. "Wait outside, Mendez," he grunted in Spanish.

"*Sí, mi general,*" Mendez replied hastily, and, as he went out and closed the door, Tam saw that the thick-set man before him had a wide, flat face, dark brown, with the flattened nose and suggestion of Asiatic slant to the eyes common to those Sonora Indians who occasionally strayed north of the border.

This must be Tamalis—General Tamalis, military head

49

of Montejo. A slight smile touched the corners of his mouth as he looked at Pedro.

"So," he said softly to Pedro, "again?" The voice was almost silken with polite satisfaction. "*Don* Tomás, I am grieved to see your friends here."

The man who stepped out from the other side of the fireplace was Tomás Cortéz. Tam felt better. Then he wondered. He had been disarmed. So had Pedro. After one look at General Tamalis he was ready to believe anything Pedro had hinted about the man. Yet what followed was staggering.

Tomás Cortéz advanced toward them, looking them up and down. He was smiling slightly also beneath his fierce white *mustachios*. "There is a mistake, *Don* Tamalis. I have never seen these men before . . . never," said Cortéz calmly, and turned to look at them again.

This fluent Spanish was hard for Tam to follow. He missed some words but got the general drift—got what Cortéz said. He had heard that a man called *don* before his last name, instead of his first, could take it as an insult.

Tamalis did. His dark face grew darker. His black mustache seemed to jerk. His smile was savage. "Look closer," he suggested. "This dog who I have met before was asking at the railroad station for you, *señor*. It was before the very door of Ruiz's house that they struck one of my brave soldiers. And they killed another when they were put under arrest."

"Killed, hell!" Tam snapped heatedly in English. "That's a dirty lie!"

Tam understood now why the bearded rancher in El Paso had said there were men who would slit their throats if Tomás Cortéz said the word. Cortéz had lied. Cortéz denied them both, left them to their fate—and Pedro took it

as a matter of course and did not even show surprise.
The officer outside looked in. Tamalis cursed him, ordered the door closed again. His hand was on the gun
under his coat. Tam tensed, waiting for that gun to come
out shooting. He'd do what he could with his hands.
But Tamalis quieted, breathing hard. "So," he said.
"You are strangers? A pity. If you were friends of *Señor*
Cortéz, I could do nothing but free you. Eh, my friend?" he
said to Cortéz.

Cortéz touched the end of his white mustache and
agreed with lazy-lidded politeness: "I am honored, Tamalis.
It is too bad I do not know them. Tell me, will they die tonight, and will you hang or shoot them?"

"Both," Tamalis said, "before I am through with them."

Tam remembered the livid scar on Pedro's arm. It
drove a chill up his back, hardened something inside to
cold fury. "Never mind that right now," he said in English.
"We came here lookin' for Miss Gray. What'd you do to
her before you sent the man who came with her out to be
shot?"

Cortéz's hand hesitated abruptly as it fingered his mustache end. His stabbing look held surprise. Tamalis did not
understand English. Cortéz interpreted, and himself asked:
"You have taken the daughter of *Señor* Gray of Guadalupe
and had her man shot?"

Tamalis answered promptly: "I have not seen the
woman. This *mazo* lies. It will not help him."

"Ah," said Cortéz. "He lies? Of course. And you will kill
them both? This American, too?"

"These *yanqui* thieves cannot come south and kill our
brave soldiers. He will die first. Presently, when our visit is
ended and we have finished these matters we discuss, I will
myself see them die."

"Perhaps," said Tomás Cortéz complacently, "I will stay and watch them."

For Tam the pot boiled over at that. He spoke to Cortéz bitterly, furiously.

"Stay an' watch, will you? Damn your dirty fat carcass! I might 'a' known you were crooked, too! Tell him you know us! Put your greasy skin in danger an' like it! If I get a bullet, I get it, but I'll let that wolf at your elbow know you're lyin'! Speak up, tell him!"

Tam ignored Pedro's hiss of warning, shook off the hand Pedro put on his elbow.

Tamalis scowled. "What does he say?" he questioned angrily.

Cortéz answered readily and smoothly. "He says, *mi general,* that man dies like a dog. But you will never know that, because a dog always remains a dog."

Tamalis's flat, dark face convulsed with rage. Jumping forward, he struck Tam in the face, raving: "*¡Tu gringo!* Myself I will kill you now!" He snatched for the gun under his coat.

Tam struck at that hard brown jaw, struck with the explosive force of pent-up rage. His hand went numb from the shock—but Tamalis was already on his way to the floor with the loose inertness of unconsciousness.

Snatching the gun from under Tamalis's coat, Tam backed to the door, covering Cortéz and Pedro. His voice lashed out at Cortéz: "Watch me get hung or shot, will you? Not tonight, *hombre!* Maybe I'll collect a little lead, but not from a firin' squad! Put 'em up, *pelado!* You, Pedro, keep out of this!" he warned Pedro in Spanish. "I know damned well now you're Cortéz's man all the way!"

The door was thick, heavy. The windows were curtained. No sound had come from the soldiers outside.

Cortéz smiled ruefully as he lifted his hands.

"Por Dios," he remarked. "You young men are all the same. You cannot wait. Old people are too slow. Softly with that gun, my young friend. If you kill Tomás Cortéz, how can he help you?"

Tam snorted. "You've got a hell of a nerve! I don't need your help! I got the bit in my teeth an' I'm on my way! Drag that skunk outta sight an' then open the door a little an' tell that gold-braided tin soldier outside that Tamalis wants him in here alone. Alone, savvy? An' close the door soon as he gets in!"

Cortéz chuckled as pulled the unconscious Tamalis aside. Then he opened the door and gave the order. A moment later Mendez stepped inside, and, as the door closed behind him, a gun muzzle dented his side.

Mendez jumped, snapped a startled oath. His jaw dropped and his hands shot up hastily when he saw Tam's cold grin behind the gun.

"I figured your tail feathers'd go down quick," Tam said. "Here, gimme that gun belt an' gun."

Mendez hastily unbuckled the gun belt and handed it over.

"Now open the door a little an' tell your men they're through here for the night. *¡Pronto!*"

Mendez stumbled in his eagerness to obey. Tam's foot stopped the door from opening more than a few inches. When the order was given and the door closed, General Tamalis was just sitting up on the floor, rubbing his jaw. Then abruptly memory came back, and Tamalis scrambled to his feet, spluttering oaths.

Tamalis had already discovered the loss of his gun, had seen where it was. Words died in his open mouth; he stood there glowering.

With the smoothness of cream Tomás Cortéz chuckled. *"Mi general,"* he said regretfully, "these young *americanos* are the very devil, no? See, with one hand this *bravo hombre* has put you on the floor, subdued me and the mighty Mendez, and to make matters worse has forced Mendez to send his brave soldiers away. Here in your great fort we are helpless."

Tamalis swelled. Veins in his forehead and neck stood out.

"Don't say it!" Tam told him coldly. "Speak when I tell you. Where's *Señorita* Gray?"

Tamalis answered sullenly. "I have not seen *la señorita* Gray."

"I think you're lyin'. Let's have it before I put a bullet in you."

The answer proved Tamalis no coward. "Shoot, and men will hear," he said. "You will not leave the fort alive. Of this *Señorita* Gray I speak no more." Tamalis folded his arms.

Tomás Cortéz chuckled again. "Let Pedro speak to our dear friend," he suggested. "They have met before."

Pedro, as if realizing that Tam wouldn't stop him, grinned broadly, put his right arm down the back of his neck and brought out a long keen knife that glittered as Pedro moved forward.

Pedro was still smiling. Something in Tam crawled as he saw that smile and remembered the long, livid scar on Pedro's arm. More like a devil than a human Pedro looked in this moment as he approached the thick-set Tamalis on the balls of his feet.

"Sí, mi general," said Pedro softly. "We meet again. It has seemed a long time. Do you remember Juana? Little Juana, who screamed while I lay dying and could not come to help her?"

With a puzzled frown Tamalis repeated: "Juana?"

"She was my sister," Pedro breathed, still smiling. "Ten thousand times since then, *mi general,* I have promised Juana the debt should be paid. But first we will hear of *Señorita* Gray."

Tamalis's voice had grown hoarse. "I do not know! Someone has lied!"

Tamalis was backing toward the fireplace. Smiling, Pedro followed until the heat stopped Tamalis. Pedro caught him by the hair and yanked his head forward.

"Oh, *sí,*" said Pedro. "Somebody has lied. And now, first, I will cut out that lying tongue. If you would save it to beg for mercy, tell where *Señorita* Gray is."

But the general was already speaking in a strangled voice, as if his tongue would not work. "Wait, I will show you!"

"Ah," said Pedro. "So. You know."

Tam was saying hurriedly to Cortéz: "You're both crazy. Tamalis'll have to get out of here. I've got it all figured out. Here, take this other gun." He knew now Cortéz couldn't be a friend of Tamalis's. The old man had been playing some sort of game.

Pedro was herding Tamalis away from the fire, his hand on the general's shoulder, the keen knife point pressing in the small of Tamalis's back.

Leaving Cortéz guarding Mendez, Tam followed Pedro across the room. Tamalis opened a door, revealing beyond the thickness of the stone partition wall, a second door barred on the side. Tamalis slid back the thick wooden bar, opened the second door, and, looking past their shoulders, Tam saw Lia Gray standing in a smaller, damp, dimly lighted room.

Lia wore a divided riding skirt and small jacket. On her

hands were still the riding gloves she had worn down from Guadalupe. She looked wan, tired, but still rebellious and without fear.

Tam took her into the next room before the fire. She cried a moment, and then smiled and wiped her eyes.

"I didn't look for anyone to come," she said. "I missed the morning train by a few minutes and the ticket man said to wait a little and he would see if there wasn't an extra train leaving. And then soldiers came and arrested us. I haven't seen Barboa since. I will remember that station agent."

"She went to school with the daughter of the president," Tam explained to Cortéz. "She figures she's got drag enough there to get some help. But her father sent me after her. I'm takin' her back."

She colored and looked defiant. "Just try it!" she snapped at him.

Cortéz slapped a fist into a palm. "She was right!" he exclaimed. "I did not know this about *Señorita* Gray. I came to Montejo to consult my friend Ruiz about this business. But it takes time. We cannot hurry. General Tamalis suspected trouble. He sent for me tonight. He was not sure about letting me go. But when Pedro came in and signed that he still had his knife, I knew he would kill Tamalis. But now, I will go to Mexico City with *Señorita* Gray, and with the daughter of the president to stand with us, we will have changes in Chihuahua quickly. The daughter of the president is the apple of her father's eye."

Maybe Cortéz was right at that. "How long before you can clear things up so the mine'll be safe?" Tam asked.

"Three days . . . four days," Cortéz answered, unconsciously prodding the wincing Mendez with his gun muzzle.

"And suppose this Bull Snyder comes down on the mine

with a heap of other men before that time an' kills off the rest?"

Cortéz shrugged. "It is the will of God," he said fatalistically.

"I thought so," said Tam grimly. "No help for the mine for three, four days. Maybe they'll all be dead by then. We aren't even out of the fort yet."

Cortéz waved a hand carelessly. "We will walk out with a gun at the head of *mi general* here. If his men try to stop us, we will shoot him. Eh?"

"I thought you had some idea like this," Tam said. "An' if you scattered his brains, where'd you be then? Shot down *pronto*. An' if you got to the train, most likely he'd telegraph ahead an' have the train stopped. If you tried to take him all the way to Mexico City with a gun at his head, you'd be in trouble *muy pronto*. An' if Pedro an' I marked him off, we'd have the whole fort after us plenty quick."

Cortéz wrinkled his brow in sudden worry. "Perhaps I am too old to think fast, after all," he admitted.

"I've got an idea," said Tam slowly. "It's crazy an' it probably won't work, but it's an idea." He spoke to Tamalis, who had been waiting limply at the point of Pedro's knife.

"How many mounted men in the fort?" Tam asked.

Tamalis licked his lips. "Forty-eight," he answered uneasily.

"Is there a big closed buggy here in town?"

"*Señor* Ruiz has one," Cortéz said.

"*Bueno.*" Tam turned to Tamalis and glared down into the dark, wide face. "Open a door an' call for an officer. Have the buggy brought to the door here, an' order every man who can ride a horse to saddle up, get his guns, an' wait outside, too."

"You are mad!" Cortéz protested. "With those men outside we will never leave here alive."

"If that's the best you can say, keep quiet," Tam said
curtly. "I'm running this now. We've got to move fast. Give
that order, Tamalis, an' God help you if you try any tricks.
Hold that knife ready, Pedro!"

VIII

The waiting that followed was the worst. They heard the
bugle calls, the shouted orders, the rising stir of activity
outside. Tamalis and Mendez stood helplessly, raging silently. Cortéz paced the floor with quick heavy steps,
wiping his brow, smoothing his white mustache ceaselessly.
Pedro waited with his knife point against Tamalis's back.

Pedro's face was a grinning mask. His eyes were like
bright coals. Tam could feel Pedro waiting for his moment
with that knife. Tamalis waited for it, too. Outside, the dis-
turbance and noise grew louder as men rode up to the
doorway and were given loud orders.

Knuckles rapped smartly against the heavy door. Cortéz
opened it a few inches. A brisk voice spoke in Spanish.
"The carriage is here. The men are ready."

"One minute," Cortéz said and, closing the door, wiped
his brow again and looked at Tam, and shrugged. "You
hear? Out there they wait with loaded guns."

Tam grinned. "We asked for it an' here it is. Miss Gray,
you take Tamalis's arm on one side an' I'll take the other.
Señor Cortéz, put out those two lamps, an' then you and
Pedro do the same with Mendez."

Save for the dying glow in the fireplace, the big room

was dark behind them as Tam stepped outside with Tamalis. Under his coat, his gun pressed hard against the general's side.

The lanterns in the great courtyard hardly gave light enough to see the carriage, the man at the open door, and the rows of mounted men beyond. Lia Gray stepped into the carriage first, Tamalis followed with Tam's hand gripping his arm. After them came the other three and the carriage was closed.

Under his breath to Tamalis, Tam gritted: "The railroad station, with all your men riding around us. Shout it out the door there an' act like you meant it."

Tamalis gagged, but gave the order, and to the thunderous clatter of two score and a half mounted men and the rumble of carriage wheels over the stone paving underfoot they passed out of the fort and down the sloping grade.

It must have been long since Montejo had seen anything like it. People crowded doorways, hung out windows, lined the narrow streets, and packed in hastily assembled crowds at the street crossings.

"This," Tam chuckled, "is somethin' I've been wanting to do all my life. Let's give the general a cheer. He deserves it." Tam put his face to the half open window and shouted: "*¡Viva General Tamalis! ¡Viva el presidente!*"

"*Carramba*, what next?" Tomás Cortéz groaned.

"Plenty." Tam chortled. "This is gettin' good." He shoved his gun out the window and shot twice into the air.

Soldiers and spectators were already shouting *vivas*. Inspired by the example from the general's carriage, the soldiers began shooting into the air, also. The noise and excitement increased as the procession traveled on.

They drew up with a flourish before a little ancient railroad station. A few guns were still blasting against the night. The train was standing ready. Faces pressed against the lighted car windows staring at the spectacle. Lia Gray looked out of her side of the carriage and gasped: "Heavens, the entire town has followed us here!"

"Let 'em come." Tam chuckled. "The more the merrier, an' with all the shootin' nobody'll ever know what happens inside here. Tamalis's goose is cooked dry an' you're all set now. *Señor* Cortéz, take the lady on the train an' get the hell off to Mexico City. We'll hang around until you pull out."

"What are you going to do?" Cortéz inquired anxiously.

"*¿Quién sabe?*" Tam said agreeably. "I'm gettin' more ideas every minute. *Adiós* an' good luck."

But Lia Gray, before she followed Cortéz out the door, caught Tam's hand. "I've never seen anything like it," she said, half laughing, half crying. "You're an utterly mad and fantastic young man, and so brave against all these odds I could cry about it. No one else would ever have thought of this. If . . . if you see my father, tell him not to worry any more than he can help."

"Sure, miss," Tam said gravely. "Don't you worry about him, either." He squeezed her firm little hand comfortingly.

In a few minutes the engine whistle blew, the bell rang, and the train pulled slowly away. When it was out of sight, Tam spoke to General Tamalis. "Tell the driver to head toward Guadalupe an' order your foreman out there to take his men back to the fort."

"It is the will of God," Tamalis gulped, and gave the order.

Once more the sun was rising hot in the morning sky when the carriage rolled through Guadalupe behind exhausted horses. It lurched slowly up to the mine office and stopped. Sandbags had been piled around the porch and the place made ready for a siege. Alexander Gray was the first man out of the door as Tam climbed stiffly down and looked around with bloodshot eyes. His face was drawn with fatigue.

Now Alexander Gray came running down the steps, calling: "I see you got her! How is she?"

"I let her go on to Mexico City," Tam said woodenly. "How's my brother?"

"Matson is holding his own," Gray replied automatically, and then his face flushed. "You let Lia go on to Mexico City, and came back in this carriage, when you could have brought her just as well?" he demanded loudly.

"That's right. Seemed to me she. . . ."

"Damn you, Matson! I don't care to know how it seemed to you! You went in my place to get her and fell down on the job! I should have known better than to send an irresponsible young fool on something like this!"

Tam answered curtly as he turned to the carriage: "That's plenty outta you, mister. I had my reasons, an' they were good enough. I brought you back a present. Pedro, run them two out here." Gun in hand, Tam stood there while General Tamalis and his brother officer got stiffly down.

The flat brown face of the general was snarling as he faced Alexander Gray. His words were venomous. "So, *señor,* you were behind this! I promise you an accounting. I was not sure . . . but now, when I get back to Montejo, I will. . . ."

Tam jabbed him with his gun. "Shut up!" he ordered in Spanish. "Maybe you won't get back to Montejo."

Gray's face was a study in surprise, then apprehension swiftly flowed over it. One could almost hear Gray thinking aloud about the final outcome of this—disaster to the mine no matter what happened now. Tamalis could—and probably would—smash them, drive them out as soon as he got back to his soldiers.

Alexander Gray's anger grew. "This is what happens from letting a young outlaw handle a delicate matter!" he burst out. "You've ruined me, Matson! Your insane actions have destroyed any chance of non-interference by the military. You'd better get your gear and get out of here while I try to patch this up."

"Not me," Tam refused coolly. "I'm stayin' here with my brother. Suit yourself about likin' it. But before you go to bowin' and scrapin' to this skunk, lemme tell you what really happened."

"I don't care to hear!"

By that time Healy and Dr. Murphy had come out. They were armed. Tam ignored them as he spoke to Gray. "You're gonna hear, an' hear plenty, mister. Don't butt in on me."

After the first moment Gray hung on the curt words which told him of the death of Barboa, the capture, the finding of Lia Gray, and all the rest of it. Gray's face grew white, then flushed again. His voice was thick, choked as he suddenly broke in. "You're telling me that this . . . this swine had my daughter locked up, and murdered Barboa, and . . . and . . . ?"

"That's right."

Gray's lashing fist was too quick to be stopped. Tamalis spun to the ground, floundered over once, sat up groggily.

"Give me a gun!" Gray shouted, snatching at the revolver Tam held. "I'll kill him here right now!"

But Pedro glided in front of Tamalis. Once more the soft, fixed smile was on Pedro's haggard face. "He is mine," Pedro warned.

Tam explained. "If there's any killin', Pedro wants it. He's met Tamalis before. Pedro had a sister that Tamalis got. Nobody got to her in time."

"I see," said Gray thickly. His face contracted in a spasm. "And you *did* get there in time. He can have Tamalis any time he wants."

"Which isn't now," Tam said promptly. "I gather Bull Snyder an' his men ain't showed up yet."

"No. But a native hunter came through Guadalupe yesterday and said he passed six Americans the day before. They were all armed heavily and riding in this general direction. They're with Snyder now, without doubt. We're expecting more trouble any time."

"You need Tamalis," Tam said. "Maybe he can threaten Snyder for you, if Snyder shows up. An' if anyone down there in the Montejo fort gets to thinkin' real hard, there's liable to be fifty armed soldiers headin' this way to see what really happened to their general. Only way we could handle 'em would be to have Tamalis alive an' kickin' to give 'em orders for us."

"That's right," Gray admitted. "We'll keep them inside here. It will be a day or so before Lia and Cortéz can get to Mexico City and do anything. Perhaps longer. In fact," said Gray heavily, "they're wasting their time. We'll get no help there. We'll do the best we can here and take what comes."

Red John was on the same cot. His face, covered with unshaved stubble now, was hollow-cheeked, feverish-looking. But he was still able to smile and talk.

"Hello, kid," Red John greeted. "I see you made it. Bring the girl back?"

To Red John, Tam sketched what had happened. Red John chuckled once or twice, but he was grave at the finish.

"Wish I had been there," he said. "Beats anything I ever heard. Made a fool outta Tamalis in his own back yard, an' carried him away in style right in front of his men. There'll be hell to pay, of course, when it gets out."

"Maybe it won't get out," said Tam.

Red John gave him a sharp look. "You're talkin' like an outlaw proper."

Tam shrugged.

"You heard what I said about this outlaw business," Red John went on slowly. "It ain't a thing for you, kid. Or any man. I oughta know."

"What should I have done down there in Montejo?" Tam asked slowly.

Red John grinned. "Just what you did. But it's what you keep on doin' that'll count. Get some sleep now."

Tam went to sleep thinking about Red John. The same thing was on Tam's mind when he woke up after dark. He had slept like one dead all day. Red John was no worse, but still helpless.

"Bull's still hidin' out," said Red John from his cot. "This oughta be good when it busts. Get some food an' help the boys keep watch tonight. An' tell that Mex' who came with you to stop edgin' around Tamalis with his knife. The general's in the front room there an' everyone's jumpin' for fear he'll be cut open the first time they turn their backs."

Pedro was meek, almost too meek about it. "Oh, *sí*," he said agreeably. "I don't hurt him at all. Oh, no. Not now."

And Pedro didn't. Not that night. Not the next day, or the next night, or the following day. Tamalis was alive. They were all alive. But the thick-set, muscular general was rapidly becoming a wreck of the man he had been. Pedro in every waking hour—and he never seemed to sleep—seemed to be lurking near Tamalis.

Men came and went on the mine shifts. Meals passed. Day followed night while they watched for the explosion to come. Nerves tightened. Isolated here from the outside world they knew to a man what would happen. The native miners were no help. No weapons were available for them, and threat of trouble from the fort at Montejo grew with each passing hour.

Red John, stronger now, was philosophizing about it. "Keep your eye peeled every minute," he warned Tam. "It's comin'. It's gonna be hell an' forked lightnin' when it hits."

And it was. . . .

IX

Darkness was an hour off when distant shots and the sharp, clear reports of gunfire drifted up from the plaza in the town. On the front porch of the mine office Alexander Gray made his decision grimly. "They're terrorizing the natives and driving them away for good, and we can't do anything about it. We must stay here together where we can help one another."

Clouds high against the blue arch of the sky were shading to purple and scarlet in the last rays of the dropping sun as Tam galloped down from the mine to see what was going on. Against the hovering quiet and the false peace of the last few days, the sharp, scattered reports of gunfire floating up from the plaza were ominous in their suggestion of what was to come.

Then, as he galloped in among the first buildings, Tam heard shots behind him, shouts, pounding hoofs back up the slope toward the mine. Reining around hard, he turned back to see a line of hard-riding men cutting across the slope toward the mine buildings. Nine of them, he counted—nine men who had been hidden around the shoulder of the hill, waiting for Red John's few remaining men to rush down into the Guadalupe plaza.

Tam was cut off from the mine office now, useless. The range was too far for accuracy. His first shot missed. His second brought down a horse. At his third shot, a man reeled in the saddle, dropped a rifle, and clutched the saddle with both hands as his horse carried him on.

Tam was in the open, visible. Two of the riders shot at him and missed. But a moment later Tam heard the dull *slap* of a bullet striking his horse high on the shoulder. The horse reared, came down uncertainly, bolted. Tam slid from the saddle and let it go. A second bullet zipped past his head into an adobe wall.

Tam ran, dodging, for the shelter of the street and houses. Another shot shrilled past his ear, and, as he turned behind the shelter of the adobe house corner, he saw his horse stagger and go down some distance away.

The gunfire around the mine was increasing. Snyder's men had reached the shelter of the long stone stable. Several of them were running on foot to the hoist house by the mine head. That would close the mine, trap the native workers underground. Bull Snyder meant business this time.

The narrow, dusty, alley-like little street between the houses rang with sound as two horsemen rode into it and galloped toward him. They saw Tam standing there and opened fire with six-guns as they came. The air was suddenly full of whining lead.

One jump took Tam to the nearest door. He kicked it in, sprang into a dim-lighted room where a cowering native woman and a brood of small children began to shriek and wail for mercy. Ignoring them, Tam slammed the door and waited beside it. The two riders galloped past, and planks ripped and splintered as guns blazed at the door. A moment later Tam stepped out.

The last rider was looking back as he rode away. He fired as Tam appeared, and his face was recognizable. It was the loud-voiced, swaggering Ben Clyde who had been in that ambush down the cañon road days before. A glow very close to contentment ran through Tam as his rifle sights came up, and they were squarely on the man.

Clyde faced forward hastily, bent low over his horse's neck, and spurred. Tam lowered the sights and squeezed the trigger. Clyde seemed to catapult out of the saddle, twisting grotesquely as he fell. He bounced, rolled over and over, and lay twisted, motionless.

Night was coming swiftly. The first hard gunfire around the mine had slackened off, but scattered shots continued without pause. Then a more ominous sound crashed out, echoing from mountain slope to mountain slope. Only exploding dynamite could have done that.

Risking himself in the open at the end of the street, Tam saw a great cloud of dust rising from one side of the mine office. For a moment he stared, and then swore aloud furiously.

Up beyond the stables a short distance, off by itself, was the low stone powder house with its locked sheet-iron door. The stable stood between it and the mine office. Snyder's men had broken into the powder house; from the shelter of the stable they were hurling dynamite sticks, with lighted fuses attached.

A second blast shook the ground as Tam looked. The geyser of earth and dust it made was a bare twenty feet from the adobe office wall. If that kept up, the earthen walls would be down around Red John and the others. Gray and his men could leave after dark—but Red John would have to stay there on the cot, helpless. Bull Snyder and his men would find him there, and that would be the last of Red John—the end of the trail for one great outlaw.

In that moment Tam sensed fully the grim threat under which Red John had lived all these outlaw years. Dashing, free, unmastered, Red John still must have ridden always with the knowledge that, when he needed mercy most, it would not be there for him. You had to grow up from a kid hero-worshipping a brother to get that sinking feeling in the middle as you stared at the violent and inevitable end awaiting him. Having a brother had to mean something to you to feel such surging, reckless anger against another man who threatened him, anger so reckless it drove you running into the open across the wide, barren slope exposed to gunfire from the mine stable.

Tam ran upright, bending only to snatch up the six-gun and rifle Ben Clyde had dropped. Plenty of ammunition was stored in the mine office, but they were short of guns. As he ran, it seemed to Tam that every man in the stable saw him at the same time and opened fire. He ran the gauntlet of a crackling roll of shots that never stopped. Bullets laced the air about him, struck the earth ahead and behind him, clipped his clothes, fanned his cheeks, whined just ahead of him until it seemed certain he would run into them each step.

But, somehow, he made it. Perhaps because Red John needed him, he made it to the safe side of the mine office and tossed the guns through an open window and scrambled after them into a haze of dust that filled the room inside. A moment later the floor shook and glass shattered in a back room from a tremendous explosion against the back corner of the building.

Red John's cot had been dragged to the most sheltered corner of the room. Red John was calm. "That last one must 'a' been two sticks," he said to Tam. "Brought a chunk of the wall down in the next room. I heard it fall. You shouldn't have come back here, kid. Gray is going to order everyone out of here after dark."

"How about you?"

The room was almost dark, but there was enough light to see Red John smile. "No time to be worrying about me," Red John said. "When they go, you get along with 'em."

"They won't get far," Tam predicted. "The horses are all in the stable. They'll be hunted down. Snyder won't want to let 'em get away."

"They'll have a chance," Red John declared. "In here they don't. Too bad Gray didn't think about that dynamite an' powder. He was sure they wouldn't damage any of the mine property. They can rush this place after dark, heave dynamite in the windows, an' blow us all into mush."

Tam went into the front room. Alexander Gray and the other men were cool and desperate. One of the women who'd come to help the doctor stood stiffly against the wall.

"It will be pitch dark very shortly," Gray said calmly. "We'll get out of here. I'm not asking any man to stay and fight. I know he'll probably be killed if he does."

One of Red John's men leaped back from the front door, yelling: "Watch out! Here's more dyn . . . !"

An ear-shattering eruption blotted out his voice. An invisible hand seemed to throw Tam back from where he stood. Glass rained about him, followed by the dull, heavy fall of great chunks of earth and the trailing scream of the woman.

A portion of the front corner had been blown in. Ominous crackings came from the roof above. Alexander Gray's warning shout was barely audible.

"Everybody in the back room! The roof is coming down!"

Tam went into the next room with the rush. In the room they had left the heavy roof corner sagged down noisily, stopped reluctantly at the height of a man's head from the floor. Dust filled the air and the whole end of the room was wreckage and chaos when they gingerly stepped back into it.

A moment later Dr. Murphy called: "General Tamalis and his man are gone!"

It was so. The two men had vanished in the excitement. Alexander Gray spoke for all of them. "I guess this means the end of us now, men. When Tamalis gets contact with his men, he'll have us hunted down like rabbits."

Gray's words were borne out; less than ten minutes later the guns in the stable quieted. An uneasy peace fell over the group of mine buildings. The voice of Bull Snyder reached them plainly.

"We're givin' you men a chance to come out of there with your hands in the air an' no guns on you! General Tamalis is here! We're a part of the Mexican army now. How does that sound, Matson? Haw-haw-haw! We're the Mex' army an' the general says to get you dead or alive! Are you comin' out?"

When there was no answer, they heard the dull *thud* of dynamite striking the ground outside. The greatest explosion of all deafened them. A ten-foot stretch of wall fell in at the top; more of the roof beams sagged down.

Tam spat dust out of his mouth. "Where's Pedro?" he called.

Pedro did not answer. He wasn't in the building when Tam looked.

"What're you goin' to do, kid?" Red John called.

"Nothin'," said Tam, and slipped through a window on the far side of the building alone a few moments later.

There was barely enough light to see close, hardly enough to betray his crouching, dodging progress as he ran along the slope, beyond the opposite mine buildings, on around the high mine dump, and up the slope above the mine.

Gasping for breath, Tam stopped in a crack above the mine. He seemed to be unnoticed. No shots came his way, and, when he was certain of that and was breathing easier, he slipped at an angle down the slope toward that small stone powder house sitting off to one side with its sheet-iron door facing up the hill.

The wind, blowing from Guadalupe across the mine office and up the slope, carried the fumes of powder smoke and dynamite, and, as Tam stopped at the corner of the powder house, he seemed to hear distant sounds like the hard, fast pound of running hoofs.

He stood, rigid, listening intently, then dropped flat and put his ear to the ground. The vibrations were there. Horses only were making that sound. Men were coming. Many men—and that could only mean the garrison from Montejo.

Grimly Tam entered the powder house. He had been inside for a few minutes the day before. In his mind lingered a clear picture of the boxes of dynamite and caps, the drums of powder, the coils of fuse.

He tore open a box of caps, cut off a length of fuse, located an open box of dynamite, slit one of the sticks with his knife, and put the cap in the end with the fuse leading out from it, risked striking a match and lighting the end of the fuse in there. He put the dynamite stick back in its box, stepped outside, and closed the sheet-iron door on the ominous *spitttt* of the burning fuse.

At that moment a panting figure turned the corner of the powder house and saw him there in the semidarkness. Tam saw a hand snatch for a belt gun. His quick dodge carried him from the door as he grabbed for his own gun. It was coming out as the other man shot at him. He was still lunging to one side as the bullet drilled him low in the shoulder, and then his own shot spun the other halfway around and dropped him. The man stirred there on the ground, groaning.

Tam's black hair prickled as he thought of the fuse burning closer to that dynamite. He started to run—and stopped, turned back, and dragged the wounded man off the ground.

"Damn fool!" Tam swore at himself as he staggered up the slope, dragging his heavy, groaning burden, crawling away from the powder house. His injured shoulder was shot with pain, every nerve stretched taut, waiting.

He had no idea how far he had gone when the burst came. An awful flash of flame made the dry gravelling hillside crystal clear; a sledge hammer blow knocked him down.

It seemed years later when Tam stirred, sat up groggily, and heard distant gunfire. Quiet lay heavy about the spot. His shoulder was wet with blood. He was badly hurt. The man he had shot lay there, without moving. Down past the stable he saw lights at the mine office, and, as he staggered to his feet, someone was shouting his name not far away.

Healy met him, speaking with relief. "What's the matter? You wounded? Here, let me help you. When that powder house blew up, it wrecked the rear end of the stable, stampeded most of the horses, broke up the attack on us, and a few minutes later the soldiers got here."

"An' so we're caught," Tam said heavily.

Healy chuckled. "I'd hardly call it that. They came up here with orders from Mexico City to protect the mine, arrest General Tamalis, and bring him back with Snyder and his men if they could be taken alive. Part of them are chasing some of Snyder's men now. Luck, eh?"

"Luck?" said Tam. "It's a miracle." He was grinning as Healy helped him into the mine office. In the wrecked front room Dr. Murphy was working over a wounded man. Pedro was lounging nearby, smoking a cigarette, and Alexander Gray was talking to a brisk young officer from Montejo.

Gray turned to them, but before he could speak, one of the Mexican soldiers tramped in behind them, saluted the officer, spoke excitedly in Spanish.

"General Tamalis has been found! They are bringing him. He was dead. In the heart he was stabbed."

"Fool!" said the young officer. "He could not have been stabbed. No one was fighting with knives. It is a bullet wound."

"*Sí, sí,*" the private assented quickly.

"Anyway," said the young officer in English, with relief, "he is dead. It makes everything easier. I will see to the body."

He hurried out with his man, and, as if by a common thought, everyone in the room looked at Pedro. Pedro's face was calm and expressionless as he looked back.

Alexander Gray cleared his throat noisily. "It doesn't matter how Tamalis died. He deserved what he got.

73

Matson, you're wounded. Get that shirt off and let the doctor get at it. Can't have anything more happen to you now. From the word that came through from Mexico City, everything is all right, thanks to your quick thinking at Montejo. You're somewhat of a hero, even if the law has been broken rather badly."

Tam grinned wryly as he started toward the rear room. "That's one for Johnny. I came down an outlaw an' I'm goin' back a hero."

Red John's snort of disgust was plain from the rear room. "I hate to punch cows with a hero," he called. "But I reckon I'll have to do it to keep you home outta trouble. Come in here, hero, an' lemme look at you."

"Comin'," said Tam, and inside once more he was warm and at peace as he walked in to join Red John.

Rodeo's "A" Man

T. T. Flynn wrote this short novel in the last two weeks in October, 1934. It was sold to Harry E. Maule, editor of *West Magazine* published by Doubleday, Doran & Co. In fact, since 1929, Maule was also editor of the Double D hard cover Westerns (the two Ds standing for Doubleday and Doran, George M. Doran having merged with Doubleday, Page & Company in 1928). The author was paid $150.00. Originally Flynn had not titled the story, calling it merely "Rodeo Western". For publication in the May, 1935 issue it was given the title it retains in this, its first appearance in book form.

I

The warden said: "You're going out of here with a clean record, Platte. I hope we won't see you in again."

A trusty clerk, typing letters over in one corner of the prison office, stopped, looked over his shoulder. Three years before, Ross Platte would not have understood the look on the trusty's face. He did now. The trusty had seen many men go out of this room in just this manner. He would see many more go out. But he would never go himself. He was doing life.

The warden was kindly. He meant well. But Ross Platte's eyes were hard and untouched.

"Thanks," he said in a voice that to his own ears was flat, toneless. "I tried to follow orders, Warden. The quicker I got out, the quicker I could find the dirty skunk who eased me in here."

The warden frowned, knit his brows. "Platte, you're on the wrong track. That idea will get you in trouble quick."

"Maybe. I'll take the trouble if I can even the score."

"Think it over," the warden said. "You're bitter now. You'll change in a little while."

They were empty words, meaningless beside forty long months, longer days, still longer nights.

"Maybe you're right, Warden," Ross Platte agreed without emotion. "We'll see." He turned to the door. The warden had one more word. "There's a visitor in the waiting room for you."

Ross stopped, frowning. "For me? I wasn't expecting anyone."

The warden was already at his desk, lifting a pen, freeing himself quickly of one more bit of responsibility. "The man seems to know who he is waiting for, Platte."

Ross Platte stepped into the grimy little waiting room warily, but the moment his eyes fell on the short, chunky man standing by the window rolling a cigarette, a broad grin spread over his face. He strode across the room.

"Rig Ranson, you moth-eaten hunk of crow-bait! I thought you were chasing cows down on the border."

Tobacco scattered on the floor, the cigarette paper fluttered unnoticed after it as Rig Ranson grabbed the extended hand.

"Me down on the border when they were fixin' to unhobble you, Ross? You oughta know better'n that, you ory-eyed son!"

They grinned as men grin at such times, to hide wordless feelings.

A sudden lump came into Ross Platte's throat as he looked down at the tanned, snub-nosed face of the man who had been his partner. Rig's last letter had come from the border country, almost a thousand miles away. Only one thing could have brought him up here to Colorado. Rig Ranson had come a thousand miles to meet Ross Platte when the prison gates opened.

Ross said gruffly: "You shouldn't have done it, Rig."

Rig answered as gruffly: "Dry up. You always did shoot your mouth off too much. Makes me plumb sick to hear you sometimes. Let's get out of this man corral before I start cussin'. Two hours has been enough to give me the jerks. When I think. . . ."

Swearing under his breath, Rig turned to the door. "We got medicine to make," he said.

The prison gate *clanged* behind them. Ross Platte had visualized it a thousand times in the past forty months. It sounded as good as he had expected. He stopped outside, threw up his head, drew a long breath.

The early spring air was crisp but the sun was bright, warm overhead. Green leaves were showing, spears of new grass pushing up from the ground. Two robins were hopping about on the ground—and ahead of them, a thousand times farther than a man could see, were neither walls nor bars to shut out the world.

He looked behind. The guard outside the gate was smiling.

"They all stop there and drink it in," the guard said. "And then half of them go on and do some damn' foolish thing to bring 'em back. Watch your step, my friend. It'll look twice as good outside there if they bring you back through this gate."

Rig snorted. "Let's get along to a drink, Ross. That bird is too cheerful for me. I got a suitcase full of your old clothes at the hotel . . . an' your riding gear an' a good horse are waiting at a livery stable in Albuquerque. I thought maybe you'd like to walk in to the hotel from here. Sort of stretch your legs."

Ross Platte grinned, drew another deep breath as he started off. "You thought right. But why the horse in Albuquerque?"

"Don't walk so fast," Rig complained. "You always was a long-legged cuss, making me rattle my pins to keep up with you. Why not Albuquerque? I guessed it'd be too coldish up here to ride out much comfortable. But it's warm down in the Río Grande valley. We can *pasear* down the valley on our own time an' get you used to a horse again. I'll bet you get saddle sores the first day out."

Ross chuckled at the idea. "Ross Platte nursing saddle sores! I wasn't aiming to head that way."

"Good a direction as any," Rig said cheerfully.

Ross Platte said slowly: "Not for me. I got things to do."

Rig grinned. "Ain't changed a bit. Always on the prod to do something. What's it now?"

Ross Platte's cheek muscles stood out as his jaw set. The tan had bleached from his face. He was thinner, softer than he had been in the old days. But harder in a different way. Ross knew he looked different. Rig had been casting covert looks at him.

"I'm going back to that little rodeo stand, Rig," Ross explained, "and find the trail of those sons-of-bitches who framed me . . . and stay on it until I catch up with them."

"Hell . . . *that?*" Rig was silent as they strode along. His face had turned grave. "Still got that on your mind, Ross?"

"Never lost it for a minute since that day in the court."

Rig didn't need details. He had been there when the judge had pronounced sentence. Ross Platte's last words to Rig as the deputy sheriff had taken him away, handcuffed, had been: "When I get out of this, I'll go after them."

Three years ago that had been, and more. The world had forgotten. Forgotten what then had been a seven-day sensation. Ross Platte, top rider of them all on the big rodeo circuit the year before, high man at Cheyenne and Pendleton, second man at Calgary, out of the game overnight and chucked into the pen because he had been convicted of stabbing a man in the back during a midnight brawl in a little one-horse rodeo town in western Colorado.

From Fort Worth to Calgary to Salinas the news had flashed along the contest circuit—and men had talked about it for a time, and gone their way and forgotten as other good riders whipped the crowds to a frenzy, took prize money, and moved on. Ross Platte had had his day. Ross Platte was gone, buried behind high walls and cold steel bars, through and done as the smiling idol of the crowds. No man who drove a knife into another man's back, reasoned Ross, could ever again draw the cheers and adulation that had once been given to smiling Ross Platte.

The smile was gone now. In its place was a hardness, a bitterness new and strange.

Rig spoke heartily: "You heard what the gatekeeper said back there."

"Every word."

"He was right, Ross."

"From his view. I've got my own."

"You don't know who all was behind that knife, Ross. You'll never catch up with 'em. Forget it."

"All I need is to hear *one man's voice*, Rig. I heard it in the dark that night. If I ever hear it again, *I'll know*."

Rig said: "There's millions of voices floating around. You could hunt years an' never hear that one again."

"It'll be on the contest circuit, somewhere, sometime."

Rig looked relieved. "Too early in the year for much of that. You listen to me. I never steered you wrong yet. You're busted, aren't you?"

"Plenty, cowboy. You peddled my horses for money to hire that shyster lawyer after you kicked in all you had."

"All right, then," said Rig. "But I saved your saddle, bridle, an' spurs. An' your riding duds. Shipped 'em down to my mother's ranch. That's where we're heading now. You ain't sat in a saddle for so long you're apt to fall off when you try it. You're soft an' you got a close-in look about you. We'll go down where you can get the feel of things again an' earn a little *dinero*."

"You ain't any better liar than you used to be, Rig. There ain't a job on your ranch. You don't need a hand . . . an' there's not a chance of me going there and living off you and your mother. Forget it . . . and thanks just the same."

"Ross," said Rig, "you're as proud and independent an' bullheaded as you always were. You used to ride me plenty and you're getting my back hair up now. Who said anything about giving you a job on the home ranch? I'm busted myself. I've got a set-up for both of us."

"It'll have to be good."

"It is. Major Lucifer Bowles an' his Bar B spread are about twenty-five miles over the mountains from us. You've heard of the major. He's been in the state fair an' rodeo game for the last twenty years. He eats it an' sleeps it."

"I've heard of him," Ross admitted. "Never met him. What's he got to do with it?"

"I met the major last year in Cheyenne, an', when the season was over, I dropped in at the Bar B. He's got a good

spread over there an' a soft spot always waiting for a good
rider. Give him the right kind of a show an' you've got a
job. An' when he goes out this year, I'll bet my leather he'll
take you along an' back you. He's got the best string of
horses in the game today."

Ross Platte's laugh held bitterness. "I've heard of Bowles
right enough. He's one of the squarest-shooting men whoever made an entry. I don't see him offering anything to
Ross Platte."

Rig rolled a cigarette in silence, flicked a match alight,
inhaled. His manner was uneasy.

"Listen, Ross," he pleaded. "There's no use climbing on
our ears about it. Maybe you're right. Bowles is a queer old
codger. But he don't know the whole story. If he knew the
truth, he'd be man enough to back you. No use going into
all that right away. He don't know Ross Platte. I been
working there since Christmas. There's no one who'll spot
you. We'll drift in, keep our mouths shut, an' say nothing
about Ross Platte. Time enough later on to bring that up."

"I'm not hiding under any other name, Rig."

"Climb down, climb down," Rig pleaded. "You need a
saddle under you an' a good horse an' lots of work. An'
some cash money later on. The Bar B has got it all . . . an' a
swing around the circuit at the end. You've got no horses
an' no money. You need backing this year. The Bar B is the
answer."

Ross Platte walked in silence for half a block, keeping his
thoughts to himself. Then spoke abruptly.

"We'll see what Bowles has to say when he gets a look at
my face. Anyway, I'll have to uncover before we go on the
road. Even if Bowles don't spot me, I couldn't get far on
the road."

Rig grinned, put a hand on his partner's arm, spoke with

relief he did not try to hide. "It's the smartest thing you ever made up your mind about, Ross. You won't regret it."

Ross Platte never knew what shaped his answer. Later he was to wonder if it was not a flashing look into the future.

"I'm not so sure about that," he said.

II

In twenty-some years a man can build up a reputation. Major Lucifer Bowles had done so, with vast enjoyment and enthusiasm. A square shooter, too square at times, a judge of horseflesh and riding, a man who made money and spent it with a free hand, who backed his opinions with cash, high, wide, and handsome. That was the major. A man who always had a ten-dollar bill in his pocket for a cowpoke down on his luck and a drink to share with him.

But this morning as the major stood beside the poles of his number three corral he was feeling aggrieved. The more so because he knew he was in the wrong.

"Dog-gone it, Joan," the major protested. "I tell you the horse is a good buy. He'll make us plenty of money this season, and you'll be glad I took a chance on him. Look at those legs and that sweep back from the neck. And that head. He's got chain lightning in his legs and heart enough to run around anything we'll meet this year."

Joan Bowles said coldly: "And you paid fifteen hundred cash for him."

The major smoothed the ends of his gray mustache and cocked a weakening eye at a hawk sailing overhead. "I've tossed more'n that away in a poker game many a time, Joanie. Now just lay off me and forget this. Slash saw this horse last year over by Las Cruces and spotted then what he could do."

"So Slash Dixon is at the bottom of this? I might have known. *Where* is Slash?"

"I don't know," said the major unhappily as he looked upon this gadfly he had sired. "And, furthermore, I don't care. I've bought the horse, paid cash for him, and I'll win it back in a few bets first race or so we put him in."

"Dad," said Joan Bowles ominously, "did you take fifteen hundred out of the note fund and pay it over for this stack of Mexican-bred crow-bait?"

"Now, Joanie. . . ."

"Don't Joanie me! What's going to become of us if you keep this up? Eleven thousand dollars due the Fifteenth of July, and we only had four thousand in the bank. And you've taken fifteen hundred of that and thrown it away on a horse I could have bought for a hundred dollars and a saddlebag full of thanks thrown in."

"You leave everything to me, Joan."

"I've left everything to you," Joan said bitterly. "And what happened? We wound up mortgaged to our ears and no way to pay out. You've thrown money away as if there was no bottom to your pocket. And the less you have, the more you spend."

"We had a few bad seasons," the major said defensively. "It takes money to make money. I had to keep going. It wasn't my fault if the men I backed didn't do so well, an' some of our horses fell down on us, and I made a few bad trades and sales. The rodeo game is coming back with a bang. There'll be money out this summer, and we'll get our share of it. I always have in the end, and I'll do it again. With Slash handling the rides and Billy Dee the roping and me trading around and handling the races, we'll come out on top this year. Slash is. . . ."

"I'm sick of hearing about Slash Dixon," Joan Bowles told her father frankly. "It's Slash this and Slash that, until the man acts as if he owned the ranch and everything on it. He's even smirking at me. He's vain, conceited, and too narrow above the nose to suit me. I'd feel better if you fired him, or at least paid less attention to him."

The major spat through the corral bars and cleared his throat. He was on firmer ground now. "Slash Dixon is one of the best riders who ever forked a saddle," he told his daughter. "An' I've seen a lot of them. I'm backing Slash this year because he'll make us money."

"Why doesn't he just go out on his own?"

"Just like a woman." The major sighed. "Contrary. You heard it all before. Slash was busted when he rode in here. I'm backing him and getting most of his prize money and any bets we can put out. Wish I had a couple more like him."

"You'd probably hire them, Dad. Slash Dixon is going to hear from me about that horse he worked off on you."

Joan stalked off toward the house. The major sighed again, and reached in his hip pocket for his plug. At times, the major thought, Joan managed to clutter up life with a lot of useless worries. Maybe Slash Dixon wasn't quite what he would have picked if money hadn't been so short. But Major Lucifer Bowles and the Bar B had a reputation to uphold. Money and plenty of it was needed this year. Slash was a rider who would help collect it. In a few months they would be out on the contest circuit. Crowds, excitement, everything that made life worthwhile would be the order of the day. The major bit off a generous corner of the plug and lifted his head like an old war horse sniffing battle afar.

★ ★ ★ ★ ★

Five days before that Ross Platte and Rig Ranson had ridden south out of Albuquerque, down the smiling Río Grande valley. Spring had come early this year to the valley. Peach trees were showing signs of bloom. The air was soft and warm, and slow-moving Mexicans were working their little irrigated valley farms. Mountains loomed on the west and east of the winding, muddy river, and, ahead, the valley stretched to El Paso.

They rode leisurely. Ross Platte's old saddle was under him—the same silver-mounted saddle he had worn smooth and shiny before cheering thousands. Rig had been right. He was soft. The first day brought aching protest from unused muscles. Then, as the warm, lazy days fell behind, Ross Platte began to tan, harden. Life, which had slowed in his body, came back with a rush.

Five days south of Albuquerque and a lazy day and a half west of the Río Grande, they rode down off the southwestern slopes of the Black Range into rolling, grassy hills, and came finally to a great wide draw cluttered with buildings at the upper end. That afternoon Ross Platte was a different man from the one who had stepped off the train at Albuquerque.

Rig pushed out his chin, Indian fashion, at the buildings and corrals ahead.

"There we are," he said. "Feel like you could handle a mean-acting pony today?"

Ross squinted into the declining sun and grinned. "Be willing to try if there's one around."

"There's the major riding up to the house now."

The major stared from the saddle at them, and then dismounted, walked into the shade at the front of the house, and waited for them.

The house was built in the style of the country—adobe, one story, with a long *portal* across the front. A short distance beyond it was a larger barn, storehouses, a windmill and concrete tank, bunkhouse and corrals, two of the corrals holding horses.

"Howdy, Major." Rig saluted as he dismounted.

The major was short, a little stooped now, leather-cheeked and somewhat seamed, with a full gray mustache stained brown around the mouth from his chewing tobacco. "Back again, Rig?" he said, but his glance was on Ross Platte and the saddle and horse Ross climbed down from. You could see the major judging the horse, eyeing the silver-mounted saddle, making up his mind about outfit and rider. And you would know, after you'd seen enough men like him, that the major was making up his mind about horse and outfit before he paid much attention to what manner of man the rider might be.

"Stayed a little longer than I aimed to, Major," Rig said cheerfully. "Meet Jack Ross, an old friend of mine. I brought Jack along to show some of your fancy riders how horse handling is really done."

The major's look was abruptly interested. "Bronc' buster, eh?" he said to Ross.

"I've ridden a few mean ones," Ross admitted.

The major pushed his gray Stetson back on his head and stroked his chin. "Mmm-mmm . . . you must be pretty good if Rig thinks so. Ever do any contest riding?"

"That's what I had in mind, Major," Rig broke in. "Somebody ought to give Ross a chance on the circuit this year. He's too good to be pushing cows around on any man's range."

The major snorted. "I've heard that kind of talk before." He hesitated. "Seen it work out now and then," he admitted. "Like to climb on an old plug back in the corral and show us some of this fancy riding? We're a bit short-handed. Might be I could use another man around here if he had the right way with horses."

Behind a screen of honeysuckle vines at the left of the *portal* a rueful chuckle reached them, and a woman spoke with an edge of sarcasm.

"I was wondering how long it would take you to weaken, Dad."

The major started and looked guilty, which was strange, Ross thought, for a man with the reputation of Major Lucifer Bowles. Hard-fisted, hard-drinking he was reputed, and here he was practically unnerved by a little sarcasm from a woman.

Then she walked out and joined them, and Ross Platte blinked and gulped and was as unnerved as the major ever had been. Shades of all that men had dreamed about in women, and written about and talked about! The world was full of women, thousands of them, good women, fine women, cluttered with looks and charm. But there was only one woman like this. Ross Platte knew it as she walked off the *portal,* and the knowledge hit him like a blow.

"Uh . . . I didn't know you were there, Joanie," the major said uncertainly. "Meet Jack Ross, maybe a good rider an' maybe not. Ross, my daughter Joan."

She was in her first twenties, no more, and she had been riding that afternoon for she wore a wool riding skirt and soft gauntlet gloves tucked in her belt. Her blouse was open on a throat smoother than the spring sunshine about them and as firm as the look she gave him. The turquoise depths of the sky above was no bluer than her eyes and the red in the gay silk handkerchief about the collar of her blouse was put to shame as a color by the faint tan on her face.

She said, smiling: "I hope you are as good as Ranson says, Mister Ross. I warn you it takes nothing short of perfection to interest Dad in a rider."

Major Lucifer Bowles looked guiltier than ever, and covered it up by smoothing the ends of his mustache and avoiding his daughter's eye.

"He's got it," Rig said flatly.

"Mmm-mmm . . . well, we better see," the major said with the same uncertainty, still avoiding his daughter's eyes. "Uh . . . won't do any harm to put a saddle on one of the horses an' look."

Ross found himself by the side of Joan Bowles as they all walked back to the corrals. How he got there he didn't know, and didn't care. Enough that he was there. She was calm, too calm when things were happening inside him that were out of his control. She gave him one direct look from those turquoise eyes.

"Been in these parts long, Mister Ross?"

"First time in, miss. But not my last. I've never seen any country that hit me so. Everything in it."

She smiled. She was amused and somehow, despite her politeness, not too glad to have him there, he sensed. Her next words held almost the same shade of sarcasm she had given her father.

"I have always wanted to see perfection in riding," she said.

"If you're expecting me to come up to Rig's boasting, you're going to be mistaken."

He couldn't keep his eyes off her as they walked side-by-side. She was totally unlike her father. Being the daughter of Major Lucifer Bowles—and what right did the old sinner have to have a daughter like this?—she would know horses and riding as only an expert could. Prison had brought a new awkwardness to him. Joan Bowles brought a new uncertainty. It had been years since he had forked a bad horse. Suppose he got pitched off quickly? There would be no excuse to stay around the Bar B. No excuse to be within sight of Joan Bowles. Ross was glad when they reached the corrals where five riders who had just come in were beginning to unsaddle.

The major called to them. "Get a saddle on Sunshine, boys, an' put him in the chute. A couple of you stand by for pick-up men. Jack Ross here is going to show us his brand of riding."

"Maybe Steamroller'd do better, Major."

The speaker was taller than Ross, slender and wiry, with a dark cast to his face that came just short of being handsome. His black sombrero was worn at a rakish angle and his fancy stitched boots and the silk handkerchief around his neck, caught through a massive silver ring, put him almost in the dude wrangler class. A thin scar from the corner of his left eye to the middle of the cheek increased his good looks, if anything, adding a suggestion of sinister dash to the handsome features.

The major hesitated. "I guess Sunshine'll do, Slash."

"What makes him think he's good enough to stick on Sunshine?"

The sneer was there, covertly veiled. Ross decided he wasn't going to like this Slash person.

The major chuckled. "If he's as good as Rig says he is, he can prove it on Sunshine. And if he does, he gets a job, Slash. You need a little competition to sharpen you up this spring."

Joan Bowles spoke under her breath. "That's Slash Dixon, Dad's top rider. Uncork a little of this perfection, Mister Ross. It might be a good idea at that if Slash had some competition."

She said the last thoughtfully. A gleam was in her eye as she looked over at the dark slim one.

III

A chute opened out of the opposite side of the corral with a level, fenced-in lot beyond. Sunshine was a strawberry roan, meek, docile, taking the saddle without protest, turning toward the chute without urging. The two pick-up men waited with grins of anticipation.

Ross grinned back at them as he slipped into the saddle and found the stirrups. No need to ask questions about Sunshine. Ross had met horses like this before. Sunshine was not a jughead, a man-hater. He was a thinker, an old, wise rodeo horse who had every trick on tap. Sunshine would be counted on to do the unexpected at the most damaging moment.

Slash Dixon stood beside the chute with a half sneer. "We're giving you something nice and soft, cowboy," he said. "If you can't make the grade on old Sunshine, you ain't any good around here."

"For a bronc' hustler who needs competition, you look mighty worried." Ross grinned down at him. "All right, give me the gate."

If he had not been looking for it, he would have lost the ride right there. The Sunshine horse's eye had been rolling back in mild interest—and the next instant better than a thousand pounds of concentrated fury went out of the chute with catapult force. It lit, stiff-legged, head down between forelegs, bucking on the run with bowed back.

The first terrific jolt drove the air from Ross's chest. The second seemed to telescope his backbone. The Sunshine horse was bucking on the run, dangerous, deadly with those terrible, bone-crushing impacts shooting up through steel-stiff legs, then, with lightning abruptness, a sudden stop in a cloud of dust, a head far down between fetlocks, and a back snapping up with all the force of a released bow string.

Dizzy and weak already, Ross stayed on and raked hard with the spurs, and the Sunshine horse snapped out of that and uncorked another mad spasm of pitching on the run, swapping ends with savage flashes of speed. It was heart-breaking. Muscles not yet hardened wrenched almost to the tearing point. If there was a ten second pick-up on this ride, it did not appear. Time had stopped. Ross felt himself growing sick. He lost one stirrup. His knees began to slip on the saddle. Then without warning the Sunshine horse soared into the air, up . . . up . . . and crashed over backwards.

Ross slid clear and lit on his feet. The ground was whirling, pitching, too. He staggered, but he had the rein and he braced himself to jump for the saddle as it came up. But, blowing hard with flaring nostrils, only a meek and docile animal got to its feet slowly and looked inquiringly about as if asking what all the fuss had been about.

One of the pick-up men rode over and caught the rein. He was grinning, but respect was there, too, now.

"Cowboy," he said, "you can *ride*. When Sunshine quit thataway, it was his way of saying he'd have to work too hard to get you off. He's a lazy cuss. Slash is the only one around here who can stick him over ten seconds. You were nearer twenty when Sunshine quit."

At the corral Rig was one big smile.

Major Lucifer Bowles was rubbing his hands together. "Not bad, Ross," he said. "Not bad at all. Mmm-mmm,

I've seen better and I've seen worse. Like to chase cows around the ranch this spring and help a little with the horses? Can't pay much, but the grub's good . . . and . . . uh . . . Joan agrees with me that we can use another man."

"You've hired a hand," Ross told the major, but he was looking at Joan Bowles as he said it.

She smiled. "You may reach perfection yet," she said. "I'll be interested to see. And so will Slash Dixon, I think."

"Mmm-mmm," said the major, reaching for his hip pocket and bringing up a formidable black plug.

The weeks raced past, jam-packed with work, hard work and not enough men to do it, not enough hours from dawn to darkness in those lengthening spring days. To talk to Major Lucifer Bowles you might not have thought it, but the Bar B ran cattle, too, on a wide-flung, scanty, dry range of owned and leased land. There were not enough men to handle the job properly.

The glamour of the rodeo arenas was far away in those long days packed with cowhand work that dirtied a man, toughened him, put steel and leather where flesh and bone had been. It was evident that money was short on the Bar B. The major was acting as his own foreman, ably seconded by Joan. Some of the men grumbled as the going grew harder, but none of them quit. Always in the background were horses and the coming rodeo season: roping, bull-dogging, broncho busting on some of the meanest outlaws Ross had ever met, and training of the slim string of running horses which in the past had put more than a sizable bet in the major's pocket.

As they went into the hot June days, practice and preparations grew more feverish.

Rig said: "Looks like the major's gonna back you, Ross."

"He hasn't said anything about it."

"He's easing you off cows a heap an' putting you with the hosses more every day. You're spending almost as much time around the home corrals here as that pain-in-the-neck, Dixon."

"He's a top rider, Rig. Joan says the major is counting a heap on him this summer."

"So it's got to be Joan and Jack," Rig said casually. "You been getting in some fast licks." Rig reached to his vest pocket for the makings. "Slash Dixon don't seem to like it," he went on. "He's gettin' a meaner look in his eye every day. I been meanin' to speak about that, Ross. There's going to be trouble there if we don't look out. Slash is layin' for you. He was point man around here until you showed up an' eased him back in the herd. He don't like it no ways."

"I'm not looking for trouble, Rig. Don't pay any attention to him."

Rig shaped his cigarette, hung it on his lower lip, and reached for a match. "I've heard talk like that before. You got to watch a rattler in your path or you'll be mighty surprised someday. Slash Dixon is a mean *hombre* even if he does look like the answer to the ladies' prayers."

"Dixon hasn't said a thing to me."

"When a rattler don't rattle, he's twice as dangerous. Watch him, Ross."

Ross stared off toward the high, wooded slopes of the Black Range in the northeast. "I don't want any trouble with Dixon that'll stop me from going out this summer," he said soberly. "I've got things to do."

"Hell, Ross, I thought you'd forgotten that."

"Forgotten it? I've been waiting."

Rig sighed. "I told you what I thought about it."

"Maybe you were right then, Rig. But you're wrong now. Plenty. How long do you think I can keep this up?" Ross Platte swept an arm fiercely at the corrals and house. His voice hardened, deepened. "They call me Jack Ross. They think I'm a drifting cowhand who wandered in here with a brand of fancy riding the major can use. They gave me a job and their friendship, an' they're trusting me more and more. How long would that last if they knew I'd walked outta prison a week before they saw me?"

"Wouldn't make any difference," Rig protested. "They took you for what you are. What difference does it make where you were before you showed up here? You can ride, can't you? You can fill the major's bill handsome. That's all that counts."

The old hard, bitter look was there on Ross's face as he answered, feelings that had been bottled up for weeks coming out. "You know damn' well that ain't all, Rig. An' so do I. How do you think I feel when the major asks me to set down on his porch in the evening sometimes, an' calls me Jack Ross, an' tells me about the contest game an' what to do an' what to look out for? Tricks I learned long ago. And Joan lets me see some of the worries she's got an' . . . an' shows she kinda likes this Jack Ross. She looks at me . . . an' I'm wondering what she'd think if she knew I was Ross Platte."

"If they knew the truth. . . ."

"They know about Ross Platte. The major dragged him out as an example of a man who could ride even if he did have a mean, yellow streak that was low enough to run a knife in a man's back when the going got tough. 'Ross Platte must 'a' been yellow an ornery clean through,' the major said. 'An I'm surprised he got as far as he did in the game before it come out!' "

94

"He was just talking, Ross."

"Talking what he thought. How do you think I felt listening to that and wondering what Joan'd say if she knew Ross Platte was there on the porch with her? Hell, I watch every stranger who rides onto the ranch, wondering if he's the one who'll recognize me. If I can get out this summer an' drag down a hunk of top money, my share'll be enough to keep me going with a chance of rooting out those skunks who framed me an' foxing the truth outta them. She'll believe it then."

"She'd believe it anyway," Rig muttered. "She ain't blind. She's had a chance to see by now you ain't like that."

"I'd hate to have to face her with it." Ross closed a fist, stared off at the mountains. "I never cared much what anyone thought about me before. But I want her to think the same as she does now after she knows I'm Ross Platte, which she's bound to do soon as we get out on the road. Somebody'll spot me there quick."

Rig spoke awkwardly. "I've got eyes, but I guess I ain't got much sense back of 'em. Sure you're right. I'm with you on it. Name the poison an' I'll drink it. An' if this Slash Dixon starts anything, I'll head him off so fast he won't know what exploded. If anyone stays behind on account of trouble, it'll be me."

"Thanks, Rig. But we'll just walk softly an' keep outta trouble."

IV

Walk softly and keep out of trouble was easy enough to say—but in the days that followed Ross Platte wondered if there was any hell on earth greater than waiting for a woman to find out a man was an imposter, his very name not his own, his real self a man she would despise as her father despised the memory of Ross Platte.

Before those stark cold facts the enmity of Slash Dixon was harmless as a vagrant summer breeze among the tortured rocks of a lava flow. Dixon could ride. Almost too well. It was queer, Ross thought in passing, that a man like Dixon should be broke and on the bounty of Major Bowles. His name should be known; he should have found other backers easily enough. But those questions did not matter before the strain of waiting for discovery and the increasing worry apparent in Joan Bowles.

Then in the last days of June, when the rodeo string was being lined up for the drive to the railroad, Joan spoke her mind. They were riding the west pasture, miles out, she and Ross alone. Joan had called to him to ride out with her, and in the first mile he had sensed she had something on her mind.

As they walked their horses along the base of a dry gravelly slope covered with low spiny clumps of *amole,* she spoke, giving him a straight sober look.

"Dad has decided to take you along, Jack."

"I was wondering," Ross said, watching how straight and proud and easily she sat in the saddle.

She was silent a moment before adding: "I wanted him to."

It might have been an unconscious move of the reins, or his horse sensing the wish in his mind, which brought them closer, so that they rode stirrup to stirrup.

"I'd rather hear you say that than anything else in the world," Ross said. He shut his mouth tightly on anything else he might say and kept his eyes ahead, also.

"What you and Slash Dixon can do will mean a lot."

"We'll do our best."

Her sudden passion was like the breaking of a dam, long strained by the flood behind it. "You've got to do more than that! More than your best! You're new to this contest game. I've seen it for years. Other men are getting ready. Scores of them. Good men. All trying to win. And only those who do, get the money. And," said Joan fiercely, "we've got to beat them to some of it! Dad's almost broke. It's been touch and go whether we'd have enough to get the rodeo outfit out on the road. He can't borrow any more. He has heavy obligations due the middle of July. Dad can run a ranch and hold his own around the contests, but he's like a child with money. For the first time since I was born he hasn't any, and he can't seem to realize it. He's living on rosy hopes. If they don't come true, he won't have any ranch to come back to or anything ahead. You and Slash Dixon are the only ones who can make those rosy hopes come true . . . and I'm not so sure about Slash Dixon. I . . . I don't like him and I don't trust him."

"And you trust me, Joan?"

"Of course."

"God bless you for that," Ross said unsteadily, and he leaned far over in the saddle and caught her around the waist and kissed her.

Joan leaned to meet him, and, when they straightened and rode hand in hand, Joan's tanned face was flushed, her blue eyes bright with a new light.

"That meant a lot to me, Jack."

"You know I love you, Joan."

"I've known. And I love you. It will be easier now, with you to share some of the worry."

Ross groaned aloud. "You've picked a mighty poor one to share it."

Joan's face was soft with an inner conviction beyond words. "I don't think so, Jack."

He kissed her again.

When they had attained a measure of soberness, he said: "I didn't know your father was that broke."

"He is, and his latest idea is to sell off two hundred of his heifers and young cows. He was offered cash for them the other day. Jay Wilson, who runs the Fishhook brand over near Alamogordo, beyond the Río Grande, wants to buy them. He knows how we're fixed and he offered a ruinous price, but he'll pay cash. All Dad can see is the cash and what he can do with it this summer. He doesn't seem to realize he'll be short of breeders next year."

"He may be right at that," Ross said thoughtfully. "If he can get through the summer and make the money he's sure of, he'll be able to pick up new breeders this fall."

"Would you sell them, Jack?"

"I think so."

"Then we'll sell," said Joan. "Let's ride back. The cattle are up in the brush now. It will take work to get them down and cull them, with all we have to do before leaving. And we have to deliver them to the Fishhook, too. That was part of the offer. It will take days to drive them over there. I don't know who to send."

"Rig and I could take them, and meet you-all out on the road."

Joan looked relieved.

"I wish you would, Jack. I'll feel better about it. We get no money until they're delivered. So much depends on it."

"They're as good as there," Ross promised.

The next few days were a mad rush of work, but finally the contrary cow critters had been rooted out of the brush, two hundred of the best culled in a mid-morning before the sharp eyes of the buyer, who departed at once.

The major looked at the herd in the fenced lot by the corrals, passed a handkerchief over his face, heaved a sigh of relief, and spoke to Ross and his daughter.

"Thank God that's done!" he said.

Ross cocked an eye at the sun. "I think I can get them off the ranch today, Major. If you'll send a couple of the boys along to hold them from breaking back tonight, Rig, Ben Green, and I can handle them from then on."

"Good idea," the major agreed. "Here comes Slash now. He can take a couple of the boys and go along. Who's that with him?"

Slash Dixon had been with the roping horses while the hot dusty work of culling had gone on. He came walking from the barn now beside another man, a shorter one, a stranger with a thin shrewd face who walked bowlegged, wore scarred leather chaps, and squinted at Ross from narrowed eyes as he came up. Something about the stranger was vaguely familiar.

The major called: "Slash . . . get a couple of the boys and help push these cows off the ranch this afternoon."

Slash Dixon looked pleased with himself. His grin was half sneer. "Sure, Major. Maybe I'd better, after what I just heard about this fellow who calls himself Jack Ross."

Ross's heart began to pump. It had come when he least expected it, in front of Joan herself, and Joan it was who asked quickly: "What do you mean by that, Slash Dixon?"

Dixon grinned at her. "This man was ridin' through and stopped at the barn. He says Jack Ross is Ross Platte, the rodeo star who knifed a fellow in the back several years ago up in Colorado and went to the pen. Kind of risky lettin' a bad one like that ride off with a couple of hundred good cows, ain't it, Major?"

V

"Damn your black dirty heart!" Ross shouted, jumping forward. His fist caught Dixon in the mouth, driving him back to the ground. Madness, blood madness, was in that blow, and in the rush that hoisted Dixon off the ground and smashed him down again. For Ross had seen Joan whiten, droop before the news as if a whip had been laid across her face.

Dixon rolled away, came up crouching, blood trickling from a split lip. He was no coward. Swearing, he rushed in, and the scar on his cheek was livid now and all the hatred he had been keeping to himself was twisting his handsome face. Ross met him willingly. They slugged toe to toe, each oblivious of everything but the savage urge to batter the other down. The major was not uncertain at times like this. His rush between them drove them apart.

"Stop it!" he bawled. "I'll have you both hog-tied an' laid out in the sun! Grab 'em, boys, an' keep 'em apart! My Lord, if they'd been packin' guns, they'd 'a' started fanning right here!"

The fracas had drawn every man in sight. Others crowded between, quiet was restored, and the major turned to the stranger.

"Who are you?" he demanded wrathfully. "What's this fool story you told Dixon?"

The squint-eyed stranger spat, scowled, shoved his old hat back on his head. "My name's Geary," he replied challengingly. "An' I told your man the truth. I don't give a burred cow's tail who believes it. I thought you all knew when I mentioned it."

Ross spoke metallically. Joan's eyes were on him, pleading, and it was to her he spoke, past the others, with a bitter pride. "He's right. I'm Ross Platte. I was in the pen. Got out this spring. Came down here to make a fresh start. My side of the story doesn't matter now. You'd better get someone else to drive your cows, Major."

At Ross's elbow Rig said furiously: "Get two more while you're at it, Major! I was Ross's sidekick when it happened an' I still am! He was framed on that deal. He never stabbed any man in the back. My chips cash in with his."

The men were muttering their surprise, staring curiously at Ross as if they had never seen him before, and the major was plainly taken aback. He fumbled at his mustache.

"Ross Platte. *Hrmmph!* No wonder you could sit a hoss. I . . . uh . . . dagnab it! Why didn't you tell me straight off? This changes the whole set-up."

Joan stepped forward. "I don't see that it does," she said. "I knew it all the time. It . . . it didn't make any difference. There's no reason why Ross Platte can't take the cattle on as he intended and then join us."

Joan's chin was up, her cheeks were flaming, and her blue eyes were defiant as she looked at them.

" 'Course not, Joanie . . . no reason at all. I . . . uh . . . you didn't say anything to me. 'Course it don't change anything," the major agreed hastily.

"No," said Joan, "it doesn't change anything. I . . . I am glad it came out like this. Ross can leave at once."

Joan hurried to the house. Ross looked dazedly after her.

Her lie had been fine and brave and convincing, even if her glance had been averted from him. A man could do anything for a girl like that. The major was speaking. . . .

"Lick, Jerry, and Tom go along with the cows. Get as far as you can before you bed 'em down. Slash, take that grub-line rider to the last fence an' see him on his way. He's cooked his goose with the Bar B by talkin' too much."

With that last shot to show where he stood, the major walked off, too. Dixon turned on his heel and accompanied the stranger to the barn.

Ross said gruffly to Rig: "We'll haze 'em out right away. Get the pack horse fixed and catch up."

He left without seeing Joan, and bedded the cows that night some miles beyond the last Bar B wire. The extra men rode back to the ranch at once. Rig unpacked, cooked a hasty supper. The three of them took turns eating. Then Ben Green, a cheerful young fellow who was all legs, long neck, and enormous Adam's apple, rolled up in his blankets for forty winks before he took his watch over the cows later in the night. Rig rode out, joined Ross, and smoked in silence some minutes.

"I'll bet," said Rig finally, "Slash Dixon knowed something when that bowlegged grub-line rider wandered in. It was timed too neat. Wasn't Slash's fault it backfired in his face."

"I knew I'd seen that fellow Geary before," Ross said. "I placed him this afternoon. He was a tinhorn gambler at Salinas about five years ago. I played some blackjack across the table from him. Didn't like him then."

"He shot his popgun today and it didn't even pop," Rig chuckled. "You should 'a' seen his face. You're sittin' pretty now. Good thing you upped and told her before."

"I didn't tell her, Rig. She was too good a sport to throw me down when I needed help. I don't know how I stand with her, and I've got a hunch there's more coming."

"How come?"

"Just a hunch."

"We'll run these cows acrost the river an' then you can roll up your sleeves and see about it," Rig said cheerfully.

Ross looked up at the stars hanging bright and near overhead, and his answer to Rig was a promise and a threat: "Don't think I won't see about it, either."

Their way lay along the western slopes of the southern tip of the range, east across a great sweep of treeless plain to the Río Grande crossing at Las Cruces, and up through the San Augustine pass in the Organ Mountains beyond. Better than a hundred and fifty miles altogether, and not much water along the way.

The second night they bedded the cattle dry on the open mesa near the old California stagecoach trail.

"We're making time," Ross said to Rig with satisfaction. "Tomorrow night we'll hit the river at this rate."

"Can't be too soon," Rig answered. "My maw raised me to punch cows, but rodeo cows are callin' right now. The major an' his outfit are ridin' a train tonight."

"In another week we'll be doin' the same," said Ross.

Rig turned in by the smoldering campfire. Ross sat by the fire smoking, listening to Rig's snores, watching the slow circling of Ben Green about the cows. Ben Green was watching until eleven, Ross until three in the morning, and then Rig would take it until the cattle came off the bed ground. By splitting up the night that way they got their rest.

Ross finally pulled off his boots, rolled in his blankets,

and dropped off to fitful sleep. Another week to go before he would have a chance to tell Joan the things that had been churning in his mind since that moment he had stood by the corrals and watched her hurry into the house.

He slept soundly—a few minutes only it seemed—and then abruptly he was throwing back the blankets, sitting up. Something had awakened him—a pistol shot he thought. But that couldn't be. None of them was wearing guns on this peaceful trip. But something had happened. The cattle were on their feet, uneasy, restless. Ross jumped up, and, as he did so, someone jammed the muzzle of a gun hard in his back.

VI

"Stand still, cowboy! Put 'em up!"

Ross froze, the last daze of sleep wiped from his brain. His hands went up. Nothing else to do. He hadn't a chance with that gun in his back.

Beyond the fire there was sudden movement as Rig sat up, and over there a rasping voice ordered: "Reach high, Shorty! I've got you covered."

"Wh-what's comin' off?" Rig stuttered.

"Your head, damn you, if you don't come outta them blankets scratchin' a star!"

Two men were riding slowly about the cows, talking soothingly. Neither of them sounded like Ben Green.

Four strangers were in sight—and a moment later a fifth spoke behind Ross.

"I guess that's got it, boys. Look for guns an' then tie them up. Watch them cows. Might be they'll take it into their heads to make a run, after all."

Rig spoke across the smoldering fire. "Ross, you over there?"

"Yep."

"What in tarnation hell is comin' off here?"

"If I had one guess, I'd say rustlers."

The gun poked his back. "You wouldn't be wrong, cowboy. Where's your gun?"

"Not a gun among the three of us."

Strangely enough the man seemed to accept his word.

Rig spoke thickly. "Rustlers? I'll be gee-totally damned! Who'd 'a' expected that, out here forty hops from Cruces an' thirty from Deming? Where's Ben Green, Ross? I dreamed I heard a shot!"

"I heard it, Rig. Out there where Ben was."

The fifth man had walked away. He rode past the campfire now and joined the two by the cattle, still poised on the brink of a stampede.

"Where's our other man?" Ross asked one of the guards.

"Shut up. Le's see what them fool cows are gonna do." After waiting a few minutes, the man grunted: "He got shot because he didn't have sense enough to stand still when he was told. Lie down on the ground there an' get yourself tied."

Ross weighed his chances. Bad. While he hesitated, the gun clubbed him behind the ear. Knees weak, head spinning, he was dragged to the ground.

A noose pinned his arms to his side and a rope was wound quickly about his body and legs. The same thing was happening across the fire to Rig. Then Rig was dragged over and one man guarded them, while the other hurried off.

Rig spoke through his teeth: "This is a helluva note!

What'll the major say when he finds his cattle's been rustled!"

Bitter was the knowledge of that. There under the stars Joan's words came back to Ross, her troubled, desperate words telling him just what the sale of these cows meant. And now. . . .

A span of horses drew a wagon to the campfire. Their blankets were tossed in the back. The two were lifted in, and a third body tumbled beside them. It laid still, one leg over Ross's leg.

Rig choked: "It's Ben Green! Dead!"

Four of the five men hazed the cows slowly off the bed ground, started them south through the night—and the wagon followed, bumping, jolting over the rough ground.

Dawn came, daylight, then the bright sun rising. They were still heading south, the cattle strung out ahead.

They had bedded the cattle not much more than six miles north of the border, six miles more and into old Mexico, into the wilds of Chihuahua where *gringo* law was jest. Once across the border the major's cows would be gone, and that sixty miles to the border lay through dry desolation where no man would be apt to see them pass.

Now and then the driver stopped, made sure the ropes were tight. Late that afternoon the cattle were watered at a windmill tank, driven off a mile or so to a bedding ground. Food was given Ross and Rig, and they were untied long enough to eat it, while a man stood watchfully behind each of them with a gun ready.

While eating, they saw Ben Green's body lashed across the back of a led horse following a rider who carried a shovel. Rig put his plate on the ground. His face was drawn, white. "I got enough," he muttered.

The man who guarded Rig shrugged, spoke indifferently through the bandanna handkerchief across his face. "Suit yourself. Back into the wagon then."

The four men had been masked when Ross and Rig emerged from the wagon. The driver had not bothered to hide his face all day, or now. He was tall, raw-boned, with a black, ragged beard. What his face looked like underneath Ross could only guess. By one thing, however, he would know the man again. The driver's left ear was crooked at the top, lopping out queerly as if the cartilage had been broken by a terrific blow sometime in the past. Shaved or unshaven he could be identified by that ear.

That night Ross tried to loosen the rope. It was tied expertly. He failed. Every little while the man standing guard looked on and inspected the knots by lantern light. Rig slept. Ross followed suit finally. There was nothing else to do.

The next day was a repetition. During the morning they passed over the International Boundary, and one of the riders yelled to the driver: "All right now, Dave! We're over the line!"

The lop-eared driver yelled: "Won't be long now!"

Ross fretted under the knowledge that the purchaser of the cattle was not looking for them for days. In all the Southwest there was no one to miss them, give an alarm.

During the day Rig asked the driver: "What are you jaspers aimin' t' do with us?"

Teeth grinned through the black beard as the driver looked over his shoulder. "Knock you over the head or put a bullet in your back, I reckon."

"Mister," said Rig, "it'd give me a heap of enjoyment to meet you out on the mesa somewhere with six-guns."

The driver chuckled. He was in high spirits, as were the

others. "For a hog-tied bull with his horns cropped an' his tail screwed up, you're makin' big talk. If I had my way, I'd see you planted in an arroyo bottom."

"Why can't you have your way?" Ross asked.

"Mebbe I will at that."

Halfway through the afternoon the herd was thrown into a circle. The wagon stopped. Men could be heard talking nearby. Some of the voices spoke broken English, mixed with Spanish. Once more what was happening was evident, although the wagon sheet cut off view.

This was the delivery point. From here Mexicans would drive the cows on south deeper into Chihuahua, probably splitting them up and scattering them.

Less than half an hour that parley lasted. Then the wagon turned north again, traveling over the rough ground without regard for the two men lying in the back. The four riders kept the driver company, singing, shouting, at times passing a bottle.

One terrific bounce threw Rig half across Ross, rolled him back again.

"Damn their low-down hides!" Rig yelled. "I wouldn't treat a polecat this way! Where do they think they're streakin' for like this?"

"Doesn't matter so much as what *we're* heading into, Rig."

"Looks like they're carryin' us back where they found us."

"Not a chance. No sense to that. We're not heading north much anyway. Look at the sun."

"That's right," Rig said, locating the sun through the wagon sheet. "We're headin' northwest. Looks like we're making for Columbus, New Mexico."

"And that," said Ross, "just plain doesn't make sense,

either. We won't do them any good around Columbus."

"You think up an answer then."

Ross had no answer. No men in their right senses would turn Rig and him loose near a border town, not with murder and rustling charges in the air. True enough, the country around that lonely, creaking windmill might be searched for months and years and no trace of Ben Green's lonely grave would turn up, but the rustling charge was enough.

The sun was setting when the mad dash into the northwest halted abruptly. The driver turned, drawled: "Boys, you're back on American ground again. Feel any better?"

Rig groaned. "I feel like hell an' I hope you do the same. This wagon bed has beat me black and blue. What's next?"

"Here's where we grub up and take it easy tonight."

"What about us?" Rig demanded.

"You'll find out about that," the driver said, climbing down.

They smelled food cooking. Dusk was thickening when they were taken out as on the preceding night, untied, led to the campfire by masked men with guns ready. They were given tin plates of food, a cup apiece of black coffee. The driver served them.

"Eat hearty, boys," he advised with grim humor. "This may be the last grub you'll stow away."

Rig sniffed the bacon and canned beans, and gulped half his cup of coffee before sitting down cross-legged on the ground. "If you figger to spoil it for me, you're talkin' out of the wrong side," he said, and attacked his food ravenously.

Ross did the same, noticing that the four men lounged about watching them. It puzzled him. The night before they had been ignored. But the food was good, the coffee welcome, and he was half starved. He wasted no time in emptying cup and plate and following Rig in a request for more coffee. They got the coffee promptly.

Rig grinned thinly over his second cup. "Looks like we're being fatted for the slaughter."

"Nice place for a slaughter," Ross commented, looking about.

Dry, sere, desolate, the country stretched to the horizon. Murder could be done easily enough here.

Rig cocked his head. "Ain't that a train whistle?"

It was far off in the north, three short blasts. It told Ross they were somewhere near the south line of the Southern Pacific, which paralleled the border along here.

Rig yawned a moment later. "The grub was good," he said. "Gosh, makes me sleepy."

No one interfered as Rig took out the makings and started to roll a cigarette, yawning several more times as he did so.

Ross yawned, too, felt his eyelids growing heavy with an overpowering desire to sleep. There was something queer about it. He saw Rig fumbling with the tobacco, saw it spill as if Rig's fingers were not working right. Ross yawned again, and his eyes closed, and he knew he was lying down to get that sleep. That was the last he knew.

VII

A hearty kick brought Ross to life. He sat up groggily. A voice was blustering above him. "I'll bend a gun over your damned head if you don't crawl out! Harrison, kick that other bum awake!"

Ross opened his eyes, which felt bleary and swollen, in time to hear another man say disgustedly: "I can't make him stir. He's still dead drunk."

"Hell, I never seen anything like it! They'll get the limit for this. They look like bad ones to me."

Stupidly Ross looked about. He was in a boxcar. A few feet away Rig lay flat on his back, sleeping heavily. Three empty tequila bottles were lying between them. The whole car reeked with the sour, woody smell of stale tequila. Outside it was getting dark.

Ross looked up at the chunky man who stood over him, poised for another kick.

"Never mind that, stranger," Ross protested. "Where are we?"

He got an oath for an answer. "Doesn't matter where you are. You're both under arrest. What's this fellow who's been guzzling with you?"

"My partner."

Open-handed slaps roused Rig.

"Wh-wha's matter?" Rig stammered thickly, struggling up.

Rig needed a shave badly, looked gaunt, hollow-cheeked in the dim light. He yawned, looked around, saw Ross. "Lord I was sleepy," he said with a wry grin. "Ain't we been kilt yet? What's this thing we're in? Looks like a boxcar."

The stocky man by Ross had a tight, hard mouth under a short black mustache. He ordered them out of the boxcar roughly. "You're both under arrest," he said. "And when you get out of jail, you'll know better than to ride freights through Del Río."

"Del what?" Rig gasped.

"Del Río."

"Texas?"

111

"Where the hell do you think? Get out of here."

"My gosh, Ross, we're clear over beyond the Big Bend, halfway across the world! Mister, what day is this?"

"Saturday night."

"An' we went off to sleep Thursday night!" Rig groaned. "It wasn't tequila done it either. I never could stand that Mex' hogwash. I wonder how quick we can get a telegram to Major Bowles an' tell him his cattle have been rustled."

"Cattle rustled? Whose cattle?" the railroad detective beside Ross demanded.

"Major Lucifer Bowles of the Bar B, outta Silver City, New Mexico," Rig told him. "We were driving some cattle of the major's an' they were rustled. The other man with us was shot dead an'. . . ."

"Better not say any more now," Ross broke in quickly.

The railroad detective grunted with satisfaction. "Cattle rustled, man killed. Looks like you two need investigatin'. I'll look into it as soon as I get you locked up. Bring him along, Harrison." He jumped down, drew a gun, and waited for Ross to follow.

Far down the track was a railroad station and beyond were houses. On the next track, on past the station, a train was standing, headlight glowing toward them in advance of darkness. Its bell began to ring, exhaust steam blasted from its stack, and it moved toward them as they started to the station with the officers.

They looked disreputable. They were dealing with hard-bitten railroad detectives. Back of Ross was that stretch in the pen. The tequila bottles were damning evidence. The major was only human. He could not be blamed if he suspected them, and over here in Texas, behind bars, nothing much could be done about it.

The oncoming train was slowly picking up speed, dragging a long string of freight cars past the station. A hand gripped Ross's right arm above the elbow. The officer plodded stolidly with his right hand in his coat pocket on the revolver. Rig's arm was also being held.

Over his shoulder, Ross asked: "How do you feel, Rig?"

"Like hell."

"Feel like a little *pasear?*"

"Huh?"

"I think we'd better see the major ourselves and explain."

"You do get the funniest ideas at the damnedest times."

Then the laboring locomotive roared past and freight cars followed in continuous rumble, drowning out any further chance of talk. Many of the freight cars were empty.

Ross tripped the man beside him, wrenched his arm loose, hooked a smashing blow as the man recovered, and snatched out his revolver. The officer went down in a heap and lay there.

Rig was already in action, arms free, fist swinging wildly. But his man was backing off, reaching under his coat. A gun appeared as Ross dove in, and, before the gun could come up, Ross's fist, driven by his momentum and the steel and leather built up by those hard weeks of riding on the Bar B, struck the man on the cheek.

The neck seemed to stretch out as the head snapped over. The man went down in a tumbling fall, rolling away from the car wheels.

No need to tell Rig what to do. He was already looking back along the train, poising himself.

An empty coal gondola rumbled swiftly up to them.

"Get it!" Ross yelled.

He sprinted alongside the train. A moment later the front of the gondola rolled past with Rig hanging onto the

113

step. Ross made a flying leap, grabbed the back hand rail, slammed against the side of the car, found the step with his high-heeled boot, and drew himself up.

Sitting on the edge of the gondola, Ross looked back, saw the two officers getting to their feet unsteadily. They waved wildly at the caboose as it sped past them, and then ran for the station.

Rig came back, grinning broadly, yelling above the train noise: "Big boy, you sure rained on 'em before they knowed it was storming."

Ross was sober. "Storm's not over yet for us."

Rig sobered, too. "Reckon not. What are we gonna do?"

"Get to the major first. Frontier Days at Prescott opened today. Tomorrow an' two more days. We'll never make it. The major said to meet them at Calgary if we couldn't. From there he's going to Sheridan, Cheyenne, and Billings. He's passing up Salinas this year."

"Ross, you got that railroad fare he gave you?"

"Not a penny. Three dollar bills, folded in my watch pocket is all. They got the rest. We'll have to bum our way and unload from this freight train quick, too. Word'll be sent ahead to look out for us."

"What are we gonna do about them cows?"

"Nothing we can do. They're gone. An army couldn't go over the line and get 'em now."

"And Ben Green?"

"Until we see the major . . . nothing."

Rig was silent a moment. "Wonder how the major'll take it about his cattle?"

"I don't know," Ross said bleakly. "I'll telegraph him first chance. But . . . hell, Rig, everything depended on the sale money. I don't even know if they'll have railroad fare or entrance money now. Joan trusted me, put everything up to me . . . an' I fell down on her."

"How much were those cows bringing?"

"Six thousand even, cash."

"Ross, my mother's got about ten thousand saved up. Insurance money. She never touches it. But . . . I could borrow six thousand. You could earn it back with a good season this year."

"Wouldn't take a cent of it! Ought to have better sense than to offer it!" Ross snapped.

Rig did have sense enough to let that subject drop. He grinned and groaned. "Oh, Lord," he said, "it's a hell of a long way to Calgary on three dollars."

One week later, two unshaven, dirty, disreputable bums unloaded from a freight train just outside Calgary, Canada, walked around the freight yards into a town packed with visitors, hung with banners, boiling with festive spirit. The great Calgary Stampede was opening next day and the world and its brother were on hand.

Ross and Rig were gaunt, hollow-cheeked, weary. Behind them lay days and nights of hard travel, long waits for freight trains, little food. The Del Río officers had evidently wired ahead. They had almost been arrested again before they got off the first freight train. Thereafter, it had seemed as if every railroad detective and law officer along the way had been watching freight trains.

Rig said: "I'm gonna borrow ten dollars somewhere an' get clean before I see the major."

"I'll find him now," Ross said. "My looks don't matter. He'll be around Stampede headquarters or out at the stables."

It was easy to locate the Bar B string. Slash Dixon was walking away as Ross came up. He gave a startled stare, stopped, scowled.

"You've got a hell of a nerve coming here!" he exclaimed.

"Where," said Ross, "is the major?"

"You don't want to see him," Slash sneered. "He's already wired Texas and New Mexico officers to arrest you on sight for stealing his cows. And . . . where's Ben Green?"

"Who said anything about Ben Green?"

"You wouldn't have got the cows if something hadn't happened to Ben Green. You're heading back to the pen again, Platte. Maybe to a hanging. Take my advice an' get out of town quick."

"Damn you an' your advice!" said Ross, heading for the stables.

Billy Dee was just jiggling one of his ropes at the stable entrance. Billy Dee's eyes widened; his rope trailed on the ground. His freckled face was first astonished, then cold.

"Hello, Platte," he said curtly.

"I'm looking for the major, Billy."

"He's lookin' for you, too," said Billy Dee. "Too bad he ain't around here with a gun. Excuse me, but I'm p'rtic'lar what I stand down wind from." He picked up his rope and walked off.

That had come from the always cheerful and friendly Billy Dee. Ross looked after him without expression, and then walked into the stable, back along the stalls, eyeing the horses.

Joan, wearing her riding costume, stepped out of one of the stalls with a bridle in one hand and a quirt in the other. She saw him, stopped. They stood at arm's length for a moment while the color drained from Joan's face and a little pulse in her throat throbbed faster, harder.

Ross said miserably: "Joan . . . you, too?"

"I didn't think you'd dare to come here," she said in a husky voice.

116

"I came to tell your father what happened."

"I don't think you had better. I don't think you had better go near him," Joan said in that husky voice.

"Joan . . . I wired him what had happened."

"Del Río, Texas, wired him what happened," Joan said. "You and Rig drunk . . . the cows gone . . . Dad's flat broke now. We came up here on prize money the boys won at Prescott. They turned their share in to Dad. To think," she said bitingly, "that I lied in front of everyone . . . told them that I knew all about you, that it didn't matter, that Ross Platte couldn't be the person everyone said he was. I know now that I thought I loved a cheat, a thief, and a liar, too cowardly even to wire the truth about what happened to the first thing of value we trusted him with. I don't even hate you. I merely despise you!"

The quirt lifted, slashed down to the sickening sound of a lash on bare flesh. Ross winced under the hot pain that brought a red welt out on the grimy stubble on his face.

Joan cried: "Get out and keep going before Dad sees you and puts you back behind bars again!"

Ross turned slowly away. "I'll wait out in front for your father. I want to tell him what happened."

He stopped there as the major himself walked into the stable, saw Ross, hurried forward. The major was red-faced, excited, redolent of whiskey, almost incoherent, with his mustache askew, one end up, the other down.

"You young hellion!" the major yelled. "Why didn't you let me know what happened? Damn my liver an' lights, you gave us a scare! Joanie, do you know what this young rascal did?"

The major clapped a hand to Ross's back, staggered slightly, hung on to Ross's arm while he waved a piece of paper at his daughter.

"No," Joan answered faintly. "What . . . what did he do?"

"Sold the cows for a thousand more than that blood sucker offered!" the major yelled jubilantly. "Here's a bank draft for seven thousand! Rig just hunted me up an' gave it to me. He says that they were both so excited they threw a drunk, climbed into a boxcar, an' woke up in Del Río, Texas, an' then took it easy getting up here to surprise us."

Ross said thickly: "Where's Rig?"

"Down town getting drunk!" the major whooped. "An' I'm planning to join him soon as Joanie takes this draft! My nerves ain't what they used to be. Hey, where you going?"

"To find Rig," Ross threw over his shoulder, and left the barn at a run.

VIII

Rig leaned on the edge of a backroom table and leered past a half empty whiskey bottle. "Fooled you," he said. "Wrote Maw from Dalhart, Texas. She had the money waitin' here. Besh lil mother I ever had. Have a drink," offered Rig sociably, shoving the bottle over. "Stoo late to lie about truth now, 'r truth about lie 'r . . . hell," stumbled Rig, "have a drink. An' then get ready to show 'em Ross Platte's back. If the crowd don' like it, make 'em like your ridin', an' if they don' like your ridin', ride like . . . hic . . . hell anyway."

Ross shoved the bottle to one side. "You damned big-hearted blundering idjit!" he said in a harsh voice that sobered Rig visibly. "Don't think I don't know what you did for me. But we're in worse than ever now. The major was too excited to ask about Ben Green. I didn't have the heart

118

to tell him in front of Joan. But . . . what about Ben Green? It's murder!"

"My gosh!" said Rig thickly. "I clean forgot 'bout Ben Green. If we sold them cows like I told the major, nothin' could 'a' happened to Ben."

"And now," said Ross, "if we go to the major with the truth about what happened to the cows, he'll figure maybe we're lyin' about that."

"Oh, Lord!" Rig groaned.

"And," said Ross, "if he believes us, he'll give the money back and they'll be broke again."

"I sure played hell, didn' I, Ross?"

"And if he believes us and keeps the money, and I'm arrested over Ben Green," said Ross, "I won't have a chance to pay your mother back."

"Ferget 'bout that."

"And if I'm arrested, you'll be, too. Because I've been in the pen once, the cards will be stacked against us all the way. We're both apt to hang."

Rig felt his neck gingerly. "I always wondered if hangin' hurt much. Never thought I might run a chance of finding out. What are we gonna do, Ross? You're sober an' got a better head than me. Get an idea quick."

"I've got one idea," Ross said seriously. "Slash Dixon gave it to me."

"Huh? Slash? All that *orejano* ever gave me was a pain."

"Dixon warned me to get out of town before I got in trouble over Ben Green."

"Nice of him."

"But I said nothing in my telegram to the major about Ben Green. Far as anyone here knows, Ben Green is back at the ranch, or ridin' around on his own business."

"Then how'd Slash get an idea to warn you?"

"That's it," said Ross. "How? He knew Ben Green was dead. He knew the cows hadn't been sold. And he was trying to help me by getting me out of town before I ran into trouble over it."

"Don' sound like Slash."

"No," said Ross, "it don't sound like Slash. He was too smooth. He wanted me on the run, out of the way. And tryin' to do that, he let slip things he shouldn't be knowing."

"I always knowed that skunk was crooked," said Rig violently. "What are you gonna do? Take a run? Or tell the major an' give yourself up? I'll go with you."

Ross said thoughtfully: "I'm not going to run . . . an' I'm not going to give myself up . . . or tell the major. It's Slash's next move. And while he's getting ready to do that, we'll enter this rodeo like everything was all right."

Rig gulped. "Y'mean we'll ride bronc's an' make a big splash while we're waitin' fer one of these Canadian Mounteds to step up an' slip handcuffs on us?"

"Just that," said Ross. "Nobody knows what happened to Ben Green but you and me an' the men who were in on rustling the major's cows. Down along the border there's no way we can cut their tracks now. They're gone. But I'm thinkin' maybe they'll leave a trail around Calgary here this week. Slash is too anxious to get us away . . . an' knows too much. We'll ride . . . an' hunt that trail."

Rig drew a deep breath, a sober breath. "Yeah," he gritted, "we'll ride an' find that trail! An' gosh help Slash Dixon if he's in on it! I'll see that he gets plenty if I have to shoot him myself!"

Joan said dolefully: "I'll always be groveling inside at the thought of that quirt on your face, Ross."

It was the next morning at the hotel. Ross and Rig had been out the night before, separately drifting around the town—Rig keeping an eye on Slash Dixon as best he could, Ross looking about. Slash Dixon had said nothing to the major about Ben Green. Joan now had no thought in her mind about it—only that quirt and the injustice which had been done.

Ross wondered what she would think and say when she heard about Ben Green. But now it was enough that she was here—like this. He needed her. Heedless of who might be passing the partly opened door, he took her in his arms.

"I had it coming for not telling you who I was first thing," he told Joan. "It didn't hurt. I knew it's only the ones we love who can hurt us enough to make us want to hurt back so hard."

Ross held her off at arm's length—and Joan smiled and said: "You're a brave boy in your arena clothes. Tell me, Ross, who bought those cows?"

He searched her face. "Why?"

"I just wanted to know," Joan said frankly. "It was so unexpected."

He had to grin at her while he furthered another lie to her. "Just like a woman . . . curious. It's a secret."

"Then I won't ask you again," Joan promised. "It's enough that you're here and everything is all right and you're going to ride today and make a big come-back. Pull them out of their seats, Ross. I'll be rooting for you . . . always."

"Always?"

"You know it, Ross. What are you thinking about? Your face looked funny then . . . hard, cold, almost despairing. It . . . it frightened me for a moment."

Ross chuckled. "I was thinking what a fool for luck I am

in having you. And what I've got to do to give you a man you'll always feel that way about and never be ashamed of."

"Foolish," said Joan, laughing. "Go out there and ride."

IX

In Calgary, under the hot July sun that day, drama began. Thousands in the stands did not know it, but hundreds did.

The announcer's hoarse voice rolled out—"Ross Platte, former rodeo star making a come-back on No Dice!"

Ross Platte. As the name percolated through the stands, a raucous voice jeered: "Take him out! Send him back where he belongs!"

Among the thousands who did not know, some clapped. Among the hundreds who did know, some gave catcalls. At the side of the chute Rig said: "He's a mean one, Ross. Just what you need. Ride him hard."

"Gate!" Ross called.

No Dice broke from the chute in an explosion of bawling viciousness and wild bucking which brought scores out of their seats and caused the judges to lean forward with interest. Riding straight up, rein high, hazing with his hat, Ross raked fore and aft for the five regulation jumps—and then continued, goading No Dice to heights of frenzy.

The old punishment was there, the spine-snapping impacts, the daze of fury and action, the seconds when it seemed that bone and flesh must fly apart and lose contact with the smooth, worn Rodeo Association saddle in the next gasping breath. But, too, the old surge and lift of the heart were there, breaking like heady wine through the gray waiting years of that Colorado interlude. The arena—the crowded stands—the fight alone in the saddle against better than half a ton of hate and fury—all wiped out for a space the feeling of disaster which was growing with every passing hour.

Then the ten second gun—the pick-up man alongside—and, as Ross went out of the saddle, a burst of cheering came from the stands.

Slash Dixon was standing by the chutes as Ross came up, and Rig chortled: "You put wings an' claws on him, cowboy! It'll take a heap of riding to top that."

Slash Dixon sneered. "Seems to me the old man is showin' a lot of forgiveness over his cows."

"Ain't you heard?" Rig asked innocently. "We pulled a trick on the major . . . didn't tell him till we got here. We sold them cows to another party for more money."

Slash Dixon spat, grinned nastily. "It makes a good story. What'll you do when pay time comes?"

Rig's grin was nasty, too. "It's come. The major's got his money. Cash. Ain't you seen him raring around here like a yearling colt?"

Slash Dixon stopped grinning, stared. "By God, you couldn't have handed him the cash. You didn't have it. You . . . hell . . . you both came in lookin' like bums."

"Which goes to show," said Rig, "you can't tell what's what from looking. Seems to me you're mighty sure we didn't sell them cows. You got any other idea what might have happened to 'em?"

The scar on Dixon's face turned color as he grew angry. His answer was almost a snarl. "How the hell should I know what happened to them? I didn't drive them off."

He walked away.

Rig squinted into the sun after him. "It was like a kick in the pants to him, Ross. He can't savvy it. You're right . . .

he knows what happened to them cows . . . an' he knows now we must 'a' paid the major for 'em . . . an' he can't make it match. I'll burr right on him," Rig promised. "He's ridin' next. Let's see how he makes out."

They watched Slash Dixon put up a good ride, almost as good, Rig admitted, as Ross on No Dice. Afterward Dixon swaggered over to the major's box in the grandstand. The major had taken a box for the week, now that he had money. It was his way.

Ross drifted over to the box a few minutes later. Slash was talking to Joan, who looked indifferent. He looked up and frowned as Ross appeared. In the box with the major and Joan were two men and two women. The major was bubbling with spirits.

"That was a great ride you put up, Ross," he greeted. "Ought to get you day money. Folks, meet Ross Platte. You've all heard of him before. Ross, this is Mister and Missus Pickett, of the Southland Stock Farms, down by Dallas. An' Dan Clancy an' Miss Hopkins."

The Picketts were plump, gray-haired, jolly, hardly like owners of a nationally known million-dollar breeding farm.

"You wouldn't believe it." Pickett chuckled, pushing back his Stetson. "But there was a day when I larruped leather like that. Luck to you, Platte. I've seen you ride before, some years ago."

He knew, of course, what had happened to Ross Platte in the last three years he had not been riding, but no hint of it appeared on Pickett's pink face.

"Thank you, sir," Ross said.

Dan Clancy was an oldish-young man, slim, dapper, with no pretense at wearing a Stetson or riding boots. Ross had crossed his trail before throughout the West. A horseman, trader, something of a promoter, Clancy was also a heavy gambler. He made big money, spent it lavishly. Ross wondered if the major was gambling with Clancy and his crowd and hoped not.

Clancy's eyes were shrewd, penetrating. "I liked your ride so well I placed two thousand on you to win the trophy, Platte. I haven't forgotten how you used to ride."

"Thanks," Ross said briefly. "I'll do the best I can."

"We know it," said the major, smoothing the ends of his mustache. "I put up a couple of thousand on you, too, Ross . . . an' I'm apt to tilt it some more."

Ross knit his brows, looked at Joan. She was smiling approval of what her father had done. His quick look caught a slight sneer at the corner of Slash Dixon's mouth. It made him wonder as he spoke to the major.

"Don't bet any more on me, Major. You never can tell what'll happen."

"I'm not worrying," the major chuckled. "I've seen you ride an' watched the others. If you have any luck with your bronc's, Clancy and I'll be in the clear."

A little later, by the arena fence, Ross said to Rig: "I didn't like the look on Dixon's face when he heard they were betting on me. He looked like he saw a tumble coming somewhere."

"I'll follow him out of the grounds," Rig promised.

Rig was back at the hotel an hour after he trailed Slash Dixon out of the rodeo grounds.

"Lost him," he said disconsolately. "He went downtown, ducked into a hotel, and slipped out through the kitchen. By the time I tracked him into the kitchen, he was gone. He acted like he smelled someone behind. Where you going?"

"Looking around for the evening. Slash Dixon isn't the only one I'm looking for here."

"I fergot." Rig smiled ruefully. "If we find everything we're looking for, we'll have our muzzles eye-deep in a mess. An' me, I get a cold shiver every time I pass one of these Mounties. I'm looking for a hand on my shoulder any minute an' a voice wanting to know what happened to Ben Green."

"Feel the same way myself," Ross admitted as he turned to the door. "We can't do anything about it. Watch for Dixon this evening."

That night, until after midnight, grim-faced and patient, Ross moved where men congregated, listening to those who spoke. And the next night, and the next, and the next.

Ben Green's name was not mentioned by anyone during those days. Slash Dixon seemed to have lost interest in the matter. Twice more Rig had lost him, but each time Dixon was in his hotel room early. Where he went, what he did, was a mystery.

Rig was seething when Ross got in late Wednesday night.

"He's worse'n a brush cow!" Rig choked. "There he is . . . an' there he ain't. An' I'll swear some *hombre* followed *me* last night. Short feller in an old gray suit. When I laid for him, he faded, too. It's getting me proddy."

"I'll follow you tomorrow night," Ross promised.

There was no trouble at the rodeo grounds. Only action. In the broncho riding, in bareback bucking, and wild steer events Ross Platte stayed in the top lists. In broncho riding he got another first, two seconds. Slash Dixon got a second and a third. The major bet another thousand on Ross. Billy Dee was leading the field in the calf roping and with his roping partner, Chuck Day, was breaking records in steer roping.

Day by day the Bar B entries had come out into the lime-light. The major was here, there, everywhere, meeting old

friends, making new ones, basking in the spotlight of attention.

Nights after the show, the major was out, also. Ross saw
him late one evening with Dan Clancy and two other men.
The next morning at the rodeo grounds Ross heard the
major chortling to Clancy over poker winnings.

Friday morning Joan said: "Ross, what is the matter?
Don't you like our company?"

Ross grinned. "Business, lady. Better tell your father to
stay in an' not play so much poker. He'll come up a loser
with the company he's keeping. Clancy and his crowd don't
play for fun."

"I've spoken to him about it, Ross. And . . . you keep
queer business hours."

Joan was smiling, but a thoughtful little frown was between her eyes as they parted.

That day Ross took another first on a mean broncho,
and that night, after the evening performance, when Rig followed Slash Dixon from the rodeo grounds, Ross was not
far behind. Dixon went downtown, merged with the
crowds. Calgary was jammed, seething with visitors from
near and far, gathering for the great wind-up on the
morrow.

If anyone was following Rig, it was almost impossible to
detect it. Then, as he kept Rig's elusive figure in sight
ahead, Ross became aware of a gray suit that seemed to be
always ahead of him, making the same turns Rig made,
stopping when Rig stopped—a short man in a gray suit.

Ross stopped watching Rig, keeping his eyes on that gray
suit. It ducked up a dark alley, was sprinting ahead when
Ross reached the alley and entered. He heard the running
steps stop. He dodged into a dark areaway out of sight.

A few moments later steps came back toward him,

walking briskly. They passed, stopped at a doorway across the alley, and, as the door opened, light from inside glanced for a moment over Slash Dixon's entering figure. The door closed; the alley was silent. It stayed that way for long minutes. Rig did not appear. Ross grew restless. At no time had Rig acted as though he had lost the trail. He should be close behind Dixon. The man in gray seemed to have been running to meet Dixon. It couldn't have been to warn him, for Slash had come on as if nothing had happened.

Ross stepped out, went on along the alley. He came to a dark intersection and stumbled over a body lying there. Swearing softly, he hurriedly struck a match. Before the match flared, Ross knew who it was. Rig, no one but Rig, would be lying there—and it was Rig, hatless, limp, with a streak of blood over his temple and a nasty gash in the scalp.

X

The gray-clad man was nowhere in sight. Rig groaned softly, stirred weakly, then sat up groggily with Ross's help.

"Wha' happened?" he muttered, and then swore and answered himself. "I was following Dixon. He turned a corner here. I snaked after him. Something moved, an' then you were holding a match in my face."

"They knew you were following Slash," Ross said. "The same man was following you. He cut around the block, ran down the alley, an' waited here. I holed up back there to see what he was up to. He dry-gulched you."

"Wait'll I get my hands on him," Rig said thickly as Ross helped him up. "Where'd he go?"

128

"Went on through the alley, I guess. But Slash Dixon went into a building back there. It's a hotel."

"Lemme at him," Rig grated.

Slash Dixon had opened the door and walked in. The two partners followed his example. Ross stepped in ahead of Rig, found himself in a short hall with doors opening off of it. One door gave into a hot, busy kitchen. Beyond that the passage turned, and a door there opened into the crowded hotel lobby.

Rig looked around disgustedly. "Might as well try to find a jack rabbit in the brush country. See him anywhere?"

Slash Dixon was not in the lobby. A bellboy standing near came over as Ross beckoned. Ross described Slash.

The boy nodded. "Yes, sir. I remember that scar on his face. He came through the door, met two men over by those chairs, and they went out the front way."

"What did the men look like?"

"One of them," said the boy, "was kind of short and bowlegged. He's staying here. The other gent'man is tall. He comes in 'most every day. One of his ears kind of turns over at the top."

Rig whistled softly. He knew about that ear.

Ross gave the boy a dollar. "Forget we asked you."

The boy palmed the dollar expertly. "I never even saw you, mister." He grinned.

Rig exploded under his breath as they walked across the lobby. "Tall, loppy-eared feller an' a short, bowlegged one! That's the grub-line rider who spilled your name at the ranch an' the wagon driver who hauled us across the border!"

"Looks thataway, Rig."

"We've got Slash tied in it now!"

"And it's not doing us any good until we find them an'

put out some bait. We know a heap now, but our word isn't any good about it. I wonder where they went?"

They were out in front now, on a sidewalk crowded with a stream of jostling pedestrians. A freckle-faced newsboy shoved a paper at Ross.

"All about the rodeo today, mister!" He peered up under Ross's Stetson. "Say, you're Ross Platte, ain'tcha, mister?"

"How so, son?"

"I've seen you ride all week. Everybody says you're the best man this year. Someday I'm gonna get on a ranch an' learn to ride that way, too."

Hero worship was there. Ross smiled as he gave the boy ten cents for a paper. "Been standing here long, son?"

" 'Bout an hour."

"I'll bet," said Ross, "you know all the good riders this year by sight."

"Pretty near all, mister."

"Know Slash Dixon, the Bar B rider?"

"Sure. He was out here a few minutes ago with two men. He shoved me back outta the way."

"Which way did they go?"

"They got in a taxi. I don't know where Joe Russell took them."

"I'd like to ride in Joe Russell's taxi, too," Ross said. "Where can I find it?"

"He'll come back here. This is his stand."

Ross parted with another silver dollar. "Show me Joe Russell when he comes back."

"I'd do it for nothing, Mister Platte."

"For a dollar," said Ross firmly, "to spend at the rodeo tomorrow."

The taxi driver said: "Sure, I took them three out to

Dewey's Inn, just outta town."

"Take us out there, too."

Dewey's Inn was a large, rambling two-story frame building back off the road among tall trees. Inside, music was playing loudly, the place was crowded, more people coming as Ross paid the driver. Their gay cow-country garb was not out of place when they went in. Half the people in sight were wearing the same.

A white-coated waiter met them. Ross described the three men. The waiter nodded. "They're upstairs in one of the private dining rooms. Number Seven. Right up the stairs there."

A noisy group entered behind Ross and Rig. A bottle shattered on the floor. A man laughed, high-pitched, penetrating. "Nemmind. Let 'er lay there. Waiter, bring another up to Room Seven!"

"Hey," said Rig, "what's the matter?"

Ross's hand had closed on Rig's arm. Ross was standing rigidly. He said huskily: "That's the laugh I been looking for! Don't turn!"

Ross looked carefully around as the group moved off. The man nearest him, the one who had laughed, was thin, stoop-shouldered, with a long face and a curious sidling walk as he started up the stairs.

"Come on," Ross said huskily, turning to the stairs a moment later.

"You look like hell an' bloody murder," Rig said.

Ross took a deep breath, relaxed, smiled mirthlessly. "It got me hard. I was thinking what that knife artist did to me three years ago. I'm all right now. They're going up where Slash is."

"Uhn-huh," said Rig colorlessly. "Slash is squattin' in every dirty corner we look into."

131

Upstairs a long hall was lined by private dining rooms. Waiters carrying loaded and empty trays hurried past them. The door of Room Seven was closed. Number Five and Number Nine on each side were occupied by noisy parties.

A sign **Reserved** hung on the door of Room Three. Ross stepped inside, closed the door. A table for six was set.

"This ain't doing us any good," Rig said. "Folks'll be in here any time."

Ross turned out the light, pushed up the window, looked out. "Let 'em," he said, throwing a leg over the sill. "There's a side porch out here, which runs clear to the back. Go down and wait out front for me."

Three-quarters of an hour later Rig was standing in the dark shadows at the side of the porch when Ross hung from the edge of the roof and dropped to the ground.

"Thought you was going to stay up there all night," Rig grumbled. "I kept looking for hell to bust loose. What now?"

"Think a heap until tomorrow night," Ross said briefly. "An' take the next dining room for tomorrow night. They're all meeting here tomorrow again at ten o'clock. Guess they've been holding out here all week. Seven of them were at the table, an' they were getting orders to bet heavy on the winner of the trophy tomorrow. I heard Slash say . . . 'Sink every dollar at the best odds you can get . . . an' then watch Platte ride to win.' "

"Slash telling 'em to bet on you?"

"Seems so."

"Don't sound right to me," Rig granted. "What about Ben Green an' the man you been looking for?"

"Tomorrow night I'll come packing a gun. Before they leave, somebody'll talk," Ross said colorlessly.

XI

Saturday—the big day. Every seat around the arena was taken. Thousands were lining the fences as the broncho riding started. Fifteen riders were in the finals.

Ross had drawn High Lonesome, a big, raw-boned black that had thrown three men during the week. Rig went to the corrals with Ross to inspect the horses.

"He's a side-winding son-of-a-gun," said Rig, peering in the corral. "The judges know it. If you stick on him, you'll get the trophy."

Behind them Slash Dixon said smoothly: "I'll be rooting for you today, Platte. Scratch him hard an' ride him handsome."

Rig bristled as he turned. "What's bringing out all this soft soap?" he demanded. "You're riding, too, ain't you?"

Slash shrugged, spread his hands, smiling. "I know when I'm licked. Platte's got the edge on me this week. Maybe better horses, maybe not. But, to even it up, I bet all my winnings on him to take top money." Slash grinned unpleasantly. "Go in and win for me, Platte," he said, and swaggered away.

"I feel like I just been kissed by a rattler," Rig snorted. "I hate winning money for a mess of skunks like that."

Handlers were putting High Lonesome into the chute when the major appeared with Dan Clancy. The major said: "Don't let anything keep you from winning today, Ross. Clancy and I have a heap of money bet on you. Clancy's nervous. He had to come over here and let you know."

Clancy was smiling as he took out a thin cigarette case, put a cork-tipped cigarette between his lips, handed one to Rig and one to Ross. "I am a little nervous," he confessed.

"You've made a great come-back this week, Platte. Everyone is talking about it. I'm backing you all the way. I guess there's no doubt you'll win, is there?"

"Never can tell," Ross said briefly.

The major snorted. "On High Lonesome, he can't help it."

"Good. I just wanted you to know I was behind you," Clancy said to Ross.

As they walked away, Ross frowned. "Don't like all this betting on me by strangers. Makes me feel like a trick mule prancing at the end of a rope."

"Ought to give you a swelled head," Rig said. "They're ready at the chute."

In the chute High Lonesome was nervous, fighting mad, with every indication of championship bucking ahead. Ross climbed the chute bars with an effort, settled himself heavily in the saddle, fitted his feet into the stirrups. For the first time that week he did not feel like championship riding. The old zest was gone.

The announcer bawled: "Ross Platte comin' out on High Lonesome to win."

The gate flew open. High Lonesome burst out of the gate with spurs against his shoulders. One . . . two . . . three jumps he made, each worse than the one before. He was a sun-fishing, slippery, twisting tornado of action. The saddle seemed slippery today, too.

Ross felt himself slipping, first one side, then the other. He gritted his teeth, held his breath—time seemed to stop— and then he started to fall. His right foot lost the stirrup. He swayed far out of balance helplessly, kicked his other foot out of the stirrup and took his first fall of the week from High Lonesome—and lost the trophy right there in a slamming, stunning impact on the ground.

When the flying heels of High Lonesome were out of the way, Ross got up groggily, walked to the chute. Rig met him, demanding: "You hurt? What happened?"

"Don't know. He was under me, an' then he wasn't."

Rig helped him back to a bale of hay. Ross sat down, head in his hands, still dizzy from the fall, heart sick at the unexpected turn of luck.

Uncertainly Rig said: "Don't take it so hard, cowboy. You couldn't stay on all of 'em. Better luck next time."

"Which isn't helping none now," Ross groaned. "The major had his roll bet on me. He'll be busted again . . . an' there wasn't any reason for me going out of that saddle. I've had worse horses this week. Seemed like I couldn't manage myself right."

"Anyway," Rig consoled, "Slash Dixon an' those other *hombres* won't enjoy their grub tonight."

Slash Dixon came up angrily. "Looks to me like you fell off that horse on purpose before I cut loose on you!"

The major, Dan Clancy, and Joan appeared. The major was downcast. Joan looked miserable, but she forced a smile. "Too bad, Ross. Don't let it worry you."

But Clancy was belligerent. His shrewd face was sneering. "That fall looked funny to me, Platte. I don't mind losing my money, but I want a run for it. I heard over in the stands that a heap of money was placed quietly this morning that you wouldn't finish the ride. Some of my money covered it. Know anything about it?"

Joan cried: "Ross, don't!"

She was too late. Ross's fist caught the gambler on the jaw. Clancy went on his back in the dirt, staggered up, holding his jaw.

"You've probably been helping the talk along!" Ross said furiously. "That's all I've got to say about it."

Men were running to the spot.

"I want to talk to you, Joan," Ross said. He took her arm, walked away with her. Back of the corrals he demanded: "You don't believe that talk, do you?"

"Of course not, Ross."

But Joan was pale, worried. Money troubles had overwhelmed her again, and more than that. She couldn't hide it. She was worried about him. The come-back of Ross Platte had taken an ugly turn. That fall from High Lonesome, rumors of advance knowledge that it would happen, could not be stopped once started.

Ross was still searching his mind for the reason of it. He had gone out of that saddle like a tenderfoot. He was still wobbly. He spoke to Joan woodenly. "Calgary seems to have made a crook out of me to a lot of people."

"It couldn't, when you aren't, Ross. Every man has his falls in bronc' riding."

"Not like I did. Not without some reason. I felt all right until I talked with your father and Clancy just before the ride . . . and after that I wasn't so good."

Joan smiled, put a hand on his arm. "Maybe Clancy put a curse on you, Ross."

Ross shook his head. "Not him. He was betting on me."

Rig hurried up. "The arena director wants to see you, Ross."

"I was afraid it would make trouble if you knocked Clancy down," Joan said miserably. "Shall I go with you, Ross, and back you up on what happened? He's fair. He'll know Clancy had no business talking like that."

"I'll talk to him alone."

The arena director was curt, his scrutiny cold. "That was a sorry ride you put up on High Lonesome, Platte. I've been hearing talk about it."

"How much do you believe?" Ross snapped.

"I don't know," the arena director said grimly. "I'm going to look into it as soon as I can get away this afternoon. And I'm warning you . . . if I find out you put up a crooked ride, I'll see that you're barred from every Rodeo Association meet in North America."

"Fair enough," Ross said bitterly. "And be damned to you and the Rodeo Association. I rode my best, and I don't know anything about these bets I hear were made today."

He walked off blazing with anger.

A cold bitterness came after the anger, lasting into the evening when the telephone rang in the hotel room. It was Joan. "Will you come down to Dad's room, Ross?" Her voice sounded tight, worried.

"Coming," Ross said.

As he hung up, Rig entered, looking dazed. "I been keeping an eye on Slash," Rig said. "Seen a man trying to pick a fight with him over something. He bet on you today an' lost to Slash. He was sore because he figured Slash knew that ride would lose. He'd heard talk."

"He lost to Slash?"

"Yeah. This morning Slash bet you wouldn't finish that ride."

Ross stood there. His hands began to work; muscles crawled, ridged in his cheeks. His voice came tonelessly. "Thanks, Rig. Stay around. I've got to see Joan a minute."

The major's room was on the floor below. Joan opened the door. She was white, the glint of unshed tears in her eyes. Back of Joan the major was pacing the floor, muttering under his breath, fumbling at the ends of his mustache with a hand that shook.

Standing by the window was the arena director, grim, hard, silent.

The major snapped, glared. "Platte," he said in a rasping, unsteady voice, "for the first time since I registered my Bar B brand before you were born, people are talking about a shady, crooked trick being hooked up with it, and maybe me. And tonight I got a letter from the ranch asking what happened to Ben Green and the horses he should 'a' brought back. It's started me thinking again. Who bought those cows, Platte? What happened to Ben . . . and what about the thousands of dollars that were bet this morning that you'd never finish that ride on High Lonesome?"

The major stopped in front of Ross, glared up at him.

Joan's eyes were pleading. Ross looked away from them, spoke in a brittle voice. "Ben Green was killed by the men who rustled your cows and ran them over the border, Major. Rig borrowed that money from his mother, for me. We were carried along with the cows, and then fed doped coffee near Columbus an' dumped in a freight car. We woke up at Del Río."

"Ross!" Joan cried. "Do you know what you're saying?"

"I know," Ross said stonily. "And I know what a crazy yarn like that means for me. Because a jury said once I stabbed a man in the back, I'll be accused of murdering Ben Green, rustling the cattle with Rig. Plenty already are saying I was mixed in with a crooked trick today."

The arena director started for the door. "This seems to be a point where the police had better be called in to start an investigation," he said curtly.

"I'm not through!" Ross snapped, stepping in front of him. "You've heard everything against me. Now stand there and hear what really happened."

They listened. At the end of it, the arena director said: "Maybe. But you can't prove any of it."

"Are you man enough, mister, to give me a chance?"

138

"I'd give a dog a chance if he was in the corner you are."

"That's all I want . . . an' here's what I need," said Ross, and he told it in a few words.

XII

That evening at twenty minutes after ten Rig spat out the window of the taxi cab that had been carrying the two of them for about an hour and a half. Rig sounded desperate as he spoke. "Lemme go back and get a hogleg an' come with you, Ross."

Ross said, as he had said many times before in that last hour and a half: "I'll do better alone."

"You'll get killed or kill a man."

"I hope," said Ross, "I get the chance."

Rig gave up, lighted a cigarette. "You're stubborn an' you'll have your way. I still ain't sure what you aim to do. But if anything happens, I'm backin' you up. Get that."

"I never doubted it," Ross said.

The taxi turned off the road. Ahead of them the bright lights of Dewey's Inn shone through the trees. If anything, a larger crowd was present tonight. As the taxi drove off, Ross said: "Wait out here. You know what to do."

"Yeah," said Rig glumly. "I know what to do . . . an' I'd a damn' sight rather be with you."

He was standing there disconsolately when Ross went inside. Downstairs a crowd was dancing. No one paid any attention as Ross went upstairs. The private dining rooms were all filled. Ross went to the door of Room Seven, opened it, stepped inside, closed the door behind him.

Voices died suddenly. Eight men around the table stared

at him, those on his side turning as they saw the others looking. A chair at the head of the table scraped back. Dan Clancy came to his feet, reddening with anger.

"What the devil are you doing here, Platte?"

They were all there, the ones who had been there the evening before—Slash Dixon—the bowlegged man who had called himself Geary—the tall man with the lopped ear, looking like a stranger now that his beard was off—the short man in the gray suit—the man whose laugh had rung for three years in Ross's mind—two strangers—and Dan Clancy.

Clancy's words brought them out of their chairs. Two men reached for hip pockets, stopped, held their hands ready.

Ross grinned coldly at them. "All here," he said. "As pretty a bunch of cut-throats an' crooks as ever was corralled."

Slash Dixon uttered an oath. The scar on his cheek was flaming. "Damn you," he said. "Get out. I warned you to leave town before the law reached out and grabbed you."

"Why didn't it, Dixon? You weren't so careful keeping secrets at the ranch when that bowlegged skunk beside you showed up with my right name. Why didn't you take that lop-eared rustler beside you and go to the police about the cattle? He could 'a' told the truth anyway."

Dan Clancy swore aloud. "Damn that ear of yours, Daniels!"

Slash Dixon showed his teeth, spoke to Clancy at the end of the table. "We might as well have it out in the open. Platte's in here now an' he ain't any man's fool. We don't want him talking."

"No," said Ross, "you don't want me talking, Slash."

White teeth gleamed, but Slash Dixon's scar was still

flaming with inner emotion. "The law didn't hear about Ben Green because we needed you this week, Platte. I was going to do what you did, but, when you showed up here, you did it better and saved a lot of talk about me."

"Meaning?"

"Meaning you went off the right horse at the right time. We don't need you now and the law does as soon as it finds out about Ben Green."

"You know I didn't rustle the major's cattle. That lop-eared skunk and maybe some of the others in the room here killed Ben and rustled the cows."

Slash laughed. "Sure they did . . . but it'll never be proved. Get this straight, Platte. The cows were rustled to get you out of the way. Instead of that, you showed up here. We made a fool out of you, got what we wanted . . . and back to the pen you go if you poke into things that aren't any of your business . . . like you did three years ago."

"I've waited three years to settle with that pasty-faced knife artist at the corner of the table, too," Ross said harshly, turning to the man. "*You,* I mean! Did you figure I wouldn't look for you?"

The thin, stoop-shouldered man sidled back from his chair, reached into his pocket. "If you're looking to open that up, Platte, you'll get a knife in you," he threatened.

Dan Clancy pounded the table. "Slim," he said angrily, "did Platte do three years for killing a man you killed?"

"He mixed in something wasn't any of his business. Started a fight. The lights went out, an' I settled it. What of it now? That's past. Settle this other business."

Clancy's oldish-young face twisted in disgust. "If I'd known that," he said, "I'd have run you out of town myself! I've done crooked things, but I never let a man spend three years behind bars for something I did!"

Slash Dixon grated: "You're going to see a man go up for a killing he didn't do, if he doesn't get out of town and keep his mouth shut."

Clancy looked sick. "When you talked me into this easy money, Slash, it looked good. I doped him with a cigarette so he lost his last ride. We cleaned up plenty on it. But when you talk about hanging Platte for killing Ben Green, that's something else again."

"He's looking for trouble. I'm giving him his chance to get out of town an' forget it. If he don't, maybe you got an idea, Clancy?" Slash sneered.

"Platte," said Dan Clancy heavily. "Take a thousand of my money and get out. You're licked."

"And if I don't, Clancy?"

The gambler hesitated.

Slash Dixon sneered again. "You hang, Platte. Clancy's got nothing to say about it. He's in this as deep as anyone."

Clancy sighed, then sat down.

"Damn you all!" said Ross. "I'm staying. I'm taking my chances with the law. When the lot of you go out of here, you'll go with handcuffs on your wrists."

"By God," said Slash Dixon, "he means it! We'll swear he came in to hold us up. Kill him!"

The lop-eared man yanked out a gun.

The door opened inward. No chance to get out quickly that way. Ross's shout drowned all sounds as he dove for the nearest man and knocked him sprawling in the dishes on the table. The next man jumped at him. Ross staggered back, smashing, ducking. The tall, raw-boned man with the lop-ear was dodging around the end of the table to get in close where he could use his gun.

Ross's fist pulped lips, shattered teeth, drove the second man back over the table. Dishes crashed on the floor. A furtive figure sidled in close. Light glinted from a keen steel blade that cut viciously up. Ross jumped back, felt the keen point slice over his left arm, deep into the flesh.

Rig had been right. He needed Rig now, a gun or a knife. There were too many of them in that small room. Warm blood was streaming down Ross's arm as he leaped back from the knife, jumped back to the end of the table where Clancy had left his chair, and made for the window.

Ross jerked Clancy's chair up, swung it with a yell. The chair legs splintered. The sidling figure that had followed him with the knife went down to the floor.

For a moment the way was cleared. A gun crashed. Ross staggered as the bullet hit his left shoulder and his whole side went numb. With his right hand he hurled the broken chair. It hit the gun, deflected a second shot. Ross caught up a beer bottle from the table, smashed the bottom on the table edge, heaved up the edge of the table against a third quick shot that splintered through an inch from his side. He followed the crashing overturn of the table and dishes, striking with terribly jagged glass edges at the hand that held the gun.

The lop-eared man leaped back with a yell, dropping the gun from a hand that spurted blood. In short seconds the room had exploded into a fury of action. From the window Dan Clancy staggered back beside Ross. His eyes were popping, his voice broke to a shrill yell of warning. "Police out on the roof! They're coming in, you fools!"

Slash Dixon grabbed for the doorknob. The door knocked him back as two men burst into the room. Two other men were clambering in through the window, grim, efficient Canadian Mounted Police.

Slash Dixon ducked under an arm, plunged out into the hall, and vanished. The two men who had come in had to let him go while they handled the others. It didn't take long. Law here north of the border was swift when it got into action. The men were lined up against the wall, except for two stretched on the floor.

Ross dropped the jagged bottleneck on the floor, picked up his trampled Stetson, lurched to the door.

"Take 'em," he said to the officers. "Tell 'em the two of you outside the window put it all down on paper an' sprung the trap I baited for 'em."

Blood was dripping in a red stream from Ross's hand as he made the hall, filling suddenly with people. From the doorway of the next room Joan met him, caught him, heedless of what happened to her dress.

"Ross, my dear! What did they do? We heard it all through the open windows, but there wasn't time to stop it."

Behind her the arena director rapped out: "Bring him in here! I'll handle him until the doctor gets here!" And he did, while Ross sat in a chair and a curious crowd jammed the doorway. "Heard everything," said the arena director gruffly as he worked. "Thought you were bluffing when you got us in here. Blasted young fool standing up there and baiting them on! Greatest thing I ever heard! I'll make it my business to set everything right about Ross Platte!"

"Everything's right now," Ross said. Joan was holding his hand. "I've got a girl I can marry."

"There never was any doubt about that," Joan said, and her eyes were misty.

In the hall a commotion grew. The major stood on a chair and looked out.

"Rig is bringing Slash Dixon back," he said excitedly.

Ross grinned weakly. "I left Rig outside to collar anyone who ran out. He finally got his hands on Slash."

"Mmm-mmm," said the major dryly. "His feet, too, by the looks. Slash's face is a mess."

"Then," Ross chuckled, "Rig's happy. I reckon there's nothing else we want."

Outlawed

T. T. Flynn did not title this story when he completed it early in July, 1935. Popular Publications had been pressuring him for more Western short novels. This story was sold on July 19, 1935 for $350. It appeared under the title "Outlawed by the Owlhoot" in *Star Western* (12/35). Subsequently it was reprinted under the title "Double Outlaw" in Popular Publications' *New Western* (7/52). For its first book appearance, the title has been changed simply to "Outlawed".

1

Coyotes were clamoring under the white moon when Ran Malone, following the faint trail left by Pardee through a notch in the low, desert ridge, saw a light glint not far ahead. Once only that light winked. It had come, Ran saw, from the window of a small adobe hut that stood there, apparently deserted, on the bare desolation of an alkali flat. Instantly he stopped his horse.

Ran pumped a cartridge into his unloaded carbine. Riding with an empty gun had been reckless and dangerous tonight. For hours each point where the shadows offered concealment had been a possible ambush. But old habits were hard to break. Ran Malone never carried a loaded rifle. He had seen a close friend die in the saddle when a gun had gone off accidentally.

Ran stubbornly followed his decisions that way. He was only twenty-six now, but the habit had become ingrained. The same characteristic had kept him on the trail of Black Pardee when other men had lost Pardee's tracks and had turned back. Ran had had a hunch that Pardee would come this way. He had circled for miles until he had again cut those tracks with the off hind hoof smaller than the others.

Now Ran sat motionless in the saddle watching the small adobe hut ahead there in the moonlight. Light did not show again. No signs of life were visible.

A full ten minutes Ran waited patiently. Then, certain he had not been observed, he dismounted. That, too, was characteristic. Wiry and straight as a stalk of ocotillo cactus, Ran had a certain stolid patience—the patience of a high-strung man who practiced iron self-control.

Ran knew what had to be done. For miles back the silver moonlight had marked the ever-increasing limp of Pardee's horse. The left foreleg was badly lamed, and getting worse. Half a mile back Pardee's boot marks had appeared in the dry sandy soil where he had been forced finally to walk and lead the horse.

That small adobe hut was as far as Pardee could have gone. The Mexican owner had been dead these several years. The country through here was deserted. A man afoot would never find another horse near here; he would be lucky to keep life in his parched, drying body. For when the witchery of the moonlight passed and the first beauty of the morning sun changed to the blistering fury of midday heat, this Por Nada country showed its fangs.

Bare hills, desert valleys, open flats where the yellow sand drifted in uneasy ripples—that was the Por Nada country. Cactus and greasewood, lizards and gaunt gray coyotes slipping through the cold, false dawn—that was the Por Nada country. Heat, loneliness and plain hell—*that* was Por Nada.

When a man's horse went lame and he was afoot at an adobe hut and a brackish well, there he stopped for an hour, a day, a week—perhaps forever. Few people rode this way; life stopped easily.

So Ran Malone knew what to expect. He led his black horse back a hundred yards where an outcropping of rocks gave cover. On a normal night the black was almost invisible, but in this flood of moonlight anything that moved was stark and clear.

Ran hobbled the black and dropped the reins, then, stooping, walking carefully, he advanced, taking cover whenever shadows permitted. The coyotes were yapping again far off beyond the low, harsh hills that raised a jagged rampart across the horizon several miles to the south. Otherwise the night was silent.

The adobe hut was quiet. Light did not show again. Gravel grated softly under Ran's high-heeled boots as he turned to the right along the slope, blending in with the ground as much as possible. He was circling wide to come at the hut from another direction. His foot loosened a small stone. It dislodged others, and the brief *clatter* grated loudly on the night.

Ran crouched motionlessly for a few moments. When no sign of life appeared at the hut, he went on. As he picked his way carefully, he wondered what Pardee was doing. Resting? Sleeping? Or peering watchfully through that single front window?

The last seemed likely. Pardee, with a price on his head for years, was as cautious and tricky as a cruising coyote, and as cold-blooded and dangerous as a coiled rattler beside a path.

There was little cover on the slope that went down to

meet the flat. Ran knew each step he took increased the danger. A watchful eye could easily see his slow circling advance. Pardee might be watching now; Pardee's rifle might be sighted; Pardee's trigger finger might be tensing for the first careful shot.

There was a cold, grim ruthlessness about Ran Malone's advance across the flat ground where the moonlight glinted on white alkali crystals. Inside, Ran felt the same way, calm and certain that this had to be done. Waiting would not help. The moon would last until the sun came up. The day would be long and hot, and the low well curbing behind the hut held life for the man who controlled it throughout the blistering day.

This end of the hut had no window. When Ran reached the point where vision from the front was cut off, he straightened, breathed a bit easier, and advanced faster on his toes toward the back of the hut. He came to the back door like a shadow drifting under the moon, put an ear to the boards, and listened. Not a sound was audible inside.

Ran was standing there with his wide, bat-wing chaps casting a grotesque shadow on the ground when a curt order sounded behind him.

"Don't move or I'll kill you!"

At the first sound Ran spun with uncanny speed. The speaker had been hiding behind the well curbing. Ran's rifle was snapping up to shoot before the voice itself registered. He was barely able to slip his finger off the trigger, and at the same moment the figure standing beside the low well curbing fired at him.

The bullet struck the top of Ran's head. He felt the dull shock of the terrific blow an instant after he realized it was a woman who had spoken, a woman who stood there in the moonlight beside the well curbing.

II

When Ran Malone recovered consciousness, the moon was still high overhead. The house was at the right, and the well curbing at his left. His head hurt terrifically.

He moved his head. A cold clear voice addressed him. "Can you understand me?"

Ran twisted his head toward the sound. The girl was standing a foot or so behind him, dressed in a divided riding skirt, a sombrero, a short jacket. The moonlight glinted on the barrel of her rifle.

Ran's face and neck were wet. She must have drawn water and slopped it over him. But his mouth was dry and parched. When he tried to sit up, he found that his ankles were bound and his wrists and elbows were lashed behind his back.

Her cold voice addressed him again. "So you will not be in doubt, understand that I will kill you instantly if you try to get free. Is that clear?"

"It oughta be," Ran replied thickly. "Do I rate a drink of water, ma'am?"

"You don't!" she said unfeelingly. "But I'll give it to you. I want to keep you alive until you hang."

Water sloshed. Her arm lifted his head. She pushed the jagged, rusty edge of a tin can against his lips. Ran drank the brackish water gratefully.

She dropped his head abruptly. The jar sent waves of pain through him. Ran winced, trying to get the straight of things. It still seemed unreasonable that Black Pardee was not standing there. Pardee should be present. He could not have gone far with his horse limping so badly, and Pardee could not have brought this woman here, either. She was a girl, slender and vigorous. When she had bent over him with the water, the moonlight had shown the smooth oval of her face. Now in the shadow cast by her sombrero brim, she looked young and pretty—too young and too pretty for this fatalistic encounter in the Por Nada country. A woman in Pardee's place was not reasonable. A woman who shot to kill as she had shot was still more unreasonable. Her cold, threatening manner raised the thing to absurdity.

"How bad is my head?" Ran asked her.

"You'll live," she answered unfeelingly. "Where are the horses?"

"Horses?"

"Exactly."

"What horses?"

"Lying won't help you!" she warned hotly.

Slow, smoldering anger drove Ran up to a sitting position. "I ain't clear as to what you're talkin' about!" he snapped. "But for a lady, you're actin' damned funny! What's on your mind?"

"I suppose you just came back to visit," she retorted witheringly.

"I didn't come back. I'd just got here."

"The man you shot in the back died half an hour later. He's in the house there." Her voice quivered for a moment. "I think the good God sent you back here to me," she said thankfully. "I think He let me see you sneaking through the moonlight."

Then Ran began to see how it was. Knowing Black Pardee, he could understand it. "I reckon," he said slowly, "a man walked in here sometime this evening leadin' a lame horse. He shot the man who was with you an' rode off with your horses."

Her reply lashed out with bitterness. "You remember

it all very well, don't you?"

"I'm guessin'," Ran said patiently. "I've been followin' that *hombre*. He's a bad one."

"Of course I don't believe you," she said. "I had gone for a walk, but after the two shots, when you rode away with all three of the horses, I was close enough to get an idea of your build and see your chaps."

"I guess there ain't any use arguin' with you about it," Ran said slowly.

"Not the slightest. But if you want to live for a little longer, tell me where those horses are. I don't intend to wander around all night looking for them."

"There's only one horse," Ran said. "Mine. Would you believe me if you saw him?"

"Your horse doesn't interest me. I saw that he was black."

Ran swore silently to himself. So Pardee had been riding a black horse, also, and wearing bat-wing chaps, too. The thing was getting more mixed up at every point.

"You're all tangled," Ran insisted. "The man you're talkin' about led a lame horse in here. It might have been black. I didn't see it. But it wasn't the black horse I rode in here."

"I think," she told him coldly, "you've said enough. Where is the horse?"

"If you find it, what do you aim to do?"

"Locate the other two horses and take you on with me."

"There aren't any more horses," Ran said flatly. "So stop arguin'."

"If I were a man, I'd make you talk!" she cried angrily. "When I think of Johnny Black, lying in there with two bullets in his back, I want to do the same to you!"

Before that picture Ran's anger melted away. For the

first time he began to realize what this girl had been up against. Crossing the Por Nada was bad enough. But to come back from a walk and find her companion dying, and the killer vanishing with the horses was little short of tragedy. She had gone through hell while the wounded man was dying. Afterward, being here alone, on foot, with a dead man for company was more than any girl should ever be called on to face. To top it all, to have a skulking shadow slip toward her through the moonlight. . . . Small wonder, Ran thought, that a touch of hysteria was in her voice. He spoke to her gently.

"You're makin' a mistake, ma'am . . . but we won't argue about it now. My horse is back there in the notch through the ridge. He's gentle. Get on him an' look around if you think I've got any more hid out."

"Leave you here alone?" she said skeptically. "Stand up. I'll release your legs."

She had tied him with rawhide thongs that she had evidently soaked in water. Now they were drying, tightening. Ran's hands were already beginning to feel numb. But he got no relief there. With the ragged edge of a tin can, she cut the rawhide around his ankles and helped him up. Standing there with his wrists and elbows lashed behind his back, Ran saw that her head barely came to his shoulder. She was so small and slight to be doing this, but there was no lack of determination in her voice as she ordered him to walk to his horse. She followed closely behind, carrying her rifle.

The black horse was standing patiently by the outcropping rocks. With only a brief word the girl brought them both back to the well. Ordering Ran to stand off a few feet, she drew water herself for the horse.

"Will he carry bareback without bucking?" she asked.

"I reckon so."

By now Ran was interested. He watched her remove the saddle, understood what was in her mind when she led the black to the well curbing.

"Get on!" she ordered coldly.

She held the horse and steadied Ran with a hand while he awkwardly mounted the well curb and slid onto the horse. Deftly she got on behind him. She left her rifle against the well curb, but she wore a heavy cartridge belt and six-gun. So armed, while Ran's hands were still behind him, she reached around him for the reins. As they rode off, she cast one look back at the lonely adobe hut.

There were times during that ride when Ran was certain hell could be no worse. His cramped shoulders and arms were strained by each movement. Pain was followed by agony, and finally numbness. The ride was silent for the most part. Their bodies were close, but a barrier separated them. The girl made no more threats, but Ran knew with certainty that she was ready to shoot him if necessary. He wondered who she was, where she was going? He asked her, and she made no answer.

The moon kept pace with them, white, cold, calm. The coyotes yapped and howled with lonely eeriness. Even the moonlight could not soften the harshness of the country.

Gray false-dawn gave way to dawn. The rose and golden hues of a gorgeous sunrise hung a mantle of beauty briefly over the desert, and the sun pushed up in a cloudless sky. The Por Nada lay about them in all its savage calm.

By mid-morning the heat lay close in shimmering fury. The black horse plodded patiently, but already it had done more than its share of traveling without rest, feed, water. Ran Malone sat on the bare, sweat-streaked back in a stupor of discomfort and pain.

"Lady," he finally said thickly, "how long do you aim to keep this up?"

"Does it matter?" she replied indifferently. "You'll hang anyway."

She spoke with an effort, as if his words had aroused her also from near stupor. Ran twisted, turning his head until he could see her face. Pale, wan, drawn with weariness, her small face was grimy with desert dust, but it was undaunted, stubbornly carrying on.

"You can't stick it much longer," Ran warned her. "It won't be long till I'll have to figure how to get you outta this."

She chuckled ironically. She could still do that.

"I'll ride as long as you do," she told him. "And when I give out, I'll make sure you don't have a chance to give orders. It's about five miles to Yaqui Pool in that lava ahead."

"Never heard of it."

"The maps don't show it. The Indians kept it a secret for a long time."

"You seem to know this country about as well as the Indians."

"I have Indian friends," she said calmly.

"Who are you?" Ran asked bluntly again.

This time she said: "My name is Anne Kilpatrick."

The name meant nothing to him. They rode in silence again and presently were threading a tortuous way through bare lava ridges that had been tumbled and piled in a great dyke by some ancient cataclysm. When it seemed to Ran that another mile would finish them both, the narrow cleft through which they were riding opened off to the right in a second gash.

Fully fifty feet high the sides of that gash rose straight up. The bottom was lava sand, cut by the marks of many hoofs. Anne Kilpatrick turned into it. A hundred yards and the gash turned left sharply, ending in a bleak lava wall that overhung the shaded sand below and a small pool of water. A dusty horse stood by the water. A man lay in the sand, sleeping. The black horse whinnied, and the sleeping man came awake and bounced to his feet, flipping out a gun.

"Looks like you've cut yourself off a hunk of trouble," Ran said thickly. "Now let's see you chew it."

Anne Kilpatrick said nothing as she steadied the black's rush toward the water.

III

Ran stared at the stranger narrowly as they rode up. What he saw was not reassuring. Stocky, powerful, with the bowed legs of a man who had spent most of his life in a saddle, the man was something of a dandy. He wore tight-fitting, soft-leather chaps, studded with polished silver *conchas,* and his leather jacket had silver *conchas* for buttons. His sombrero was high-crowned, in the style of the country south of the border, and a braided band of silver wire ran around the base of the crown.

The horse was a magnificent gray animal, bearing a fine, silver-trimmed saddle. But Ran's glance fastened on the dark, suspicious face that watched them. The stranger wore two gun belts. A repeating rifle leaned against the rock wall within arm's reach.

This was no rancher, no cowman passing through the Por Nada. The signs were there for a knowing man to read. No kindness, gentleness, or mercy showed in the harsh lines of the bold face. But Ran did his best.

"Hi-yah!" he called.

The man looked startled, suspicious at what he saw. Then a slow, broadening grin came over his face. The wary tenseness went out of his manner.

"I'll be damned if I didn't think I was seein' things! Lady, where'd you get this buzzard you're packin' around so careful?"

"That doesn't matter, does it?" Anne Kilpatrick replied coolly. "Help him down. We both need water badly."

She was sawing on the bit to keep the horse from plunging into the water. The man thrust out a stubby, powerful hand and forced the frantic animal back.

" 'Light an' make yourself comfortable, miss," he said with exaggerated politeness. "It ain't often a pretty girl like you shows up in country like this."

She slipped softly to the ground and stood back while Ran slid off. Ran staggered. She steadied him. Her grip was unexpectedly firm and strong.

"Water the horse first, please," she told the man, and Ran forgave her a lot when she said that.

Grinning, the stranger let the horse drink.

"That's enough," Ran told him a moment later.

That got him a quick glance of annoyance. "For a man who's tied up like a turkey cock headin' for market, you've got a heap to say," the stranger grunted. He pulled the horse from the water and stood with a sardonic smile while they drank.

Ran felt better as he stood up and faced the man's estimating stare. Still grinning sardonically, the other spoke to Anne Kilpatrick.

"Where'd you get this *hombre*? Where you takin' him?"

"He shot a man in the back. I'm takin' him to the law."

"You don't say?" The man's eyebrows lifted in exaggerated surprise. "Plugged a man in the back, eh? He must be a bad one. But you're sure takin' a heap of trouble to get rid of him, miss. Whyn't you shoot him an' save the trouble?"

"He'll have a fair trial."

"That's just your pretty little soft heart workin'," the stranger said, grinning. "Now me, I ain't that way. Suppose I put a bullet in him, plant him in the sand, an' that'll be the end of it?"

"Thanks. I'll handle him my way."

Ran's face set in bleak lines. "We're gettin' along, stranger. Let the lady mind her own business."

For an answer he got a full-handed blow to the jaw that knocked him sprawling. A kick followed.

"You're talkin' too much," the stranger told him, thumbing back the hammer of his gun.

Ran struggled to his knees. He saw Anne Kilpatrick, holding her revolver, noticed how small was her hand. Without much hope he heard her sharp warning.

"Get away from him!"

The man looked at her with a scowl, and then laughed shortly. "Put that gun up before you hurt yourself!" he ordered.

"You heard me!"

"I'd shore hate to hurt such a pretty little thing. Gimme that gun." He stepped toward her, putting out his hand.

Anne Kilpatrick backed away. He followed. Her back came against the dark lava rock, and she was cornered.

Ran was on his feet again by then. He made a lumbering rush. The man turned on him, uttering an oath. Anne Kilpatrick swung her big revolver and struck. The stranger dropped where he stood.

A moment later Ran was standing over the unconscious

man, saying gruffly: "This ain't no way to act now. You oughta be proud."

For Anne Kilpatrick was standing there, trembling. "I thought I'd have to kill him," she said unsteadily.

"Good riddance if you had."

"But I . . . I've never killed anyone. I don't want to!"

Ran had to laugh. "For a girl who mighty near blew the top of my head off an' has been raising conniption fits all over the Por Nada, you're showin' a mighty tender side. Buck up an' get this jasper's gun off him before he comes to."

Ran stood there with little quizzical lines at the corners of his eyes while she disarmed the unconscious figure. She was steady again when she finished.

"Maybe it was a good thing," she said with an attempt at perkiness. "We need his horse. I'll send men back for him."

"It's a good idea." Ran nodded. "But a better idea'll be to loosen this rawhide around my arms. Gangrene'll be settin' in. Maybe it's too late already. If I am goin' to hang, it'll look better if I jump off with both arms."

She searched his face, nodded, and with the stranger's hunting knife slashed the hard, dry rawhide thongs.

For minutes Ran's arms remained useless. Then he groaned as circulation crept back. The rising pain was exquisite torture.

Anne Kilpatrick stood to one side with her gun cocked. When Ran began to swing his arms and finally to rub them vigorously, she said: "Can you ride now?"

"Plenty. Can you?" Ran grinned.

"I'll follow you on his horse. And . . . I'll shoot if I have to."

Ran looked at her quizzically. "I believe you," he agreed.

"It'll hurt you more'n it does me . . . but you'll shoot. All right. I'll remember that."

They were on the horses, ready to leave, when the stranger sat up groggily. He felt the side of his head, then saw them and scrambled to his feet, reaching for a gun. But Anne Kilpatrick had all his weapons.

"Don't forget there's a lady present, an' I ain't tied up now," Ran warned him.

The man stood there, legs braced in the sand, glaring at them. "You aim to leave me here on foot?" he asked harshly.

"You're already left," Ran said indifferently. "I'd leave you on your belly to crawl if I had the say. But the lady's soft-hearted. She's gonna send men back for you. I'd advise you to fill up on water an' start walkin'. She's a grizzly, an' her men'll have claws."

"How's a man to walk outta this god-forsaken hole?" the stranger yelled furiously.

"You figure it out." Ran grinned. "*Adiós, amigo*. I got to get along an' get hung." Ran lifted a hand in a parting salute as he swung his horse around and started off.

Troubled, Anne Kilpatrick spoke when they were out of sight. "I don't like to leave him there like that. After all. . . ."

"After all," said Ran, "he brought it on himself. You're too soft-hearted at the wrong times."

"You're a queer man," she said thoughtfully, behind him. "You tried to help me back there."

"I don't pick on women . . . or shoot men in the back."

She said nothing to that. In a little while they were out of the lava, again riding through the pitiless blast of the sun. But the water, the brief rest, the extra horse, made a world of difference. They traveled faster, easier. But at that the heat would have dropped any ordinary woman; the country would have daunted many men. South they bore toward low mountains that looked as barren and harsh as this lower country.

Late in the afternoon they struck a pair of wagon ruts, and followed these ruts into the low mountains as the sun went down. Winding, twisting, traveling steeply upward, they kept on. Thirst gripped Ran again; hunger gnawed. And if he felt that way, how did Anne Kilpatrick feel? The bare rocks about them offered no relief. But when they finally gained the crest and started down the other slope, the moon showed signs of greater rainfall. Stunted trees reared in grotesque shapes on the rocky slopes; cactus grew more plentiful; scanty grass began to appear.

They rode down a narrow, winding cañon and presently a trickle of water appeared beside the trail and grew more plentiful as they advanced. They stopped, drank, and rode on in the silence of sodden weariness.

A dozen times Ran could have escaped. He did not. It was too much like taking advantage of an exhausted child. He was beginning to wonder if, left alone, she could go on. Finally he spoke over his shoulder.

"You're killin' yourself. How much more of this do you aim to try?"

"Keep on," she ordered wearily.

Not long after that the cañon widened out. The moonlight showed a greener, fairer country rolling gently ahead to the faint twinkling of lights.

They followed the shallow little stream for another hour—and suddenly they were there, riding up to cottonwoods, corrals, a windmill, and buildings of a ranch.

Dogs met them, barking, and quieted when Anne Kilpatrick spoke. Men came out of the house and waited for them.

"The dogs act like you belong here," Ran commented.

"This is the YK ranch. My two brothers and I own it," the girl answered shortly.

There was no more time for speech as they rode to the house and Anne Kilpatrick called: "Bill, I've got a prisoner. He killed Johnny Black and I brought him in."

Other men appeared around the end of the house, hurrying toward them. Ran slipped from the bare back of his horse, saying calmly: "Never mind the guns, men. All I want is some sleep right now."

A voice answered with harsh amusement. "You'll both get a place to sleep. I never thought we'd have a lady with us tonight. Grab 'em, boys!"

IV

A gun was in Ran's side. It would have been futile to resist. Four men were around him already, all with guns out.

He stood still while Anne Kilpatrick struggled briefly, was overpowered, disarmed. Then he spoke coolly.

"Pardee, ain't that you?"

"What's that? Who'n hell are you?"

"Ran Malone!"

Pardee stepped over and peered at Ran's face. He was a good three inches taller, broader, thicker, and now the situation struck him as a huge joke.

"If I didn't see it, I wouldn't believe it!" he chortled. "Ran Malone herded in here like a cactus-fed maverick! Boys, here's an *hombre* every sheriff in the Nueces River

162

country is boogery over, an' damned if a woman ain't made him chew bait an' come a-crawlin'!"

They laughed.

"What's wrong with them Nueces lawmen? Ain't they as good as a woman?" one man asked.

"Nothin' the matter with the sheriffs," Pardee retorted jocularly. "Malone must 'a' tamed down a heap."

Anne Kilpatrick said: "So he *is* an outlaw!"

"Lady," said Black Pardee, turning toward her, "he ain't no preacher's boy. Where'd you get him?"

"He shot a man who was with me, and took our horses."

"You don't say?" returned Pardee, with a new note of interest in his voice. "Where'd all this happen?"

"Out in the Por Nada. And will you please tell me," said Anne Kilpatrick with a challenge that was almost pathetic now, "what are you doing here? Where is my brother?"

"They're all takin' things easy for a while. We've sorta taken charge of the ranch, you might say, ma'am," Pardee said with mock politeness.

"My brother . . . did you . . . is he hurt?"

"If you mean that lank son-of-a-gun that calls himself Bill Kilpatrick, he's cussin' strong when he can use his mouth, ma'am. Only his left arm is shot up a little. Bring 'em in the house, boys."

Seven men, including Pardee, gathered about them in the big, lamp-lighted living room. They were hardcases. Pardee looked as big, as hard, as dangerous and ruthless as ever. The man was all bone and muscle inside his bat-wing chaps, his riding boots, his shirt opened over a thick neck. He wore a calfskin jacket and a single gun. Somewhere about him would be the deadly little Forty-One caliber Derringer he always carried. But you never really knew Pardee by looking at his black mustache, his narrow, thin-lipped mouth, his sharply ridged nose. The slightly slanting eyes under bushy black brows, the dark-skinned, saturnine cast of the face topped off with coal-black hair inclined to be curly, did not give the reason why the man was called Black Pardee. But when you saw once the savage black temper of the man, you knew. Pardee's fits of murderous fury made him worse than the common run of killers. Yet now Pardee was almost genial as he looked at Anne Kilpatrick and showed white teeth in a smile of appreciation.

"Ain't she a sight for sore eyes, boys?"

They agreed. A short, bandy-legged man with a hooked nose, said solemnly: "She's the purtiest ever I seen!"

Anne Kilpatrick looked too weary to have any emotion. "I want to see my brother," she said to Pardee.

"Shore, ma'am. I'll take you myself."

She went with him calmly, unafraid outwardly. Ran looked after them, scowling. He had heard stories about Pardee and women.

The minutes before Pardee returned dragged. No mock politeness was in his manner once he did. He was grim as he opened a sack of tobacco and started to build a smoke.

"Well, Malone," he said, staring over the cigarette, "it's shore a hell of a surprise to see you here. How come?"

Ran shrugged. "Things got a little warm on the Nueces."

Pardee moistened the paper, shaped the cigarette, reached in his vest for a match. "Never got too warm for you before," he said, flicking the match alight with a thumbnail.

"Any reason why I shouldn't travel?" Ran asked calmly.

"Nope," said Pardee, dribbling smoke through his nose. "But there ain't any good reason why you should light around here. Funny you bein' in the Por Nada just now.

The girl says you plugged the fellow she was ridin' with. He was the foreman here. That don't sound like you, Malone. You always put up a smooth front." Pardee sneered slightly.

"My front ain't changed," Ran said calmly. "I didn't shoot the fellow. I rode into the Por Nada after a ranny who held up a stage. When I seen a light in a house, I figured it was him an' I eased up close to make sure. She was hidin' out behind the well. She creased me, an' had me tied when I came out of it."

Ran showed the blood-soaked wound on his head.

Pardee stared in frowning concentration. He was no fool.

"Why was you after the man who held up the stage?" Pardee asked. "You packin' a badge now?"

"I came along just as the posse was startin' out. So I rode along. Me bein' a stranger on a strange range, I figured he might be someone I could do business with. I was driftin' on west anyway."

"So you had to sneak up on him, huh?"

"Him expectin' a posse, it seemed to be a good idea to get the drop on him first an' talk afterwards." Ran grinned. "Only the girl got the drop on me. She swore I'd killed her partner an' hazed me on here."

But Pardee still was not satisfied. "If she was afoot out there in the Por Nada, where'd that extra horse come from?"

"I had an extra horse," Ran said calmly.

Suddenly Pardee was not suspicious. "You played in luck, Malone. If we hadn't been here, they'd shore have hung you. Likely the fellow you was trailin' is outta these parts by now."

"Likely," Ran agreed with a straight face. "How long are you gonna keep me standin' here with a gun in my back?

I'm thinkin' we can do business. You ain't squattin' on this ranch for fun."

"Correct," said Pardee. "We can use a man as handy with a gun as you are, Malone. You want to throw in with us?"

"What's the play?"

"No hurry. You'll get told later."

"All I want right now is grub an' a place to sleep."

"Cheyenne, take him in the kitchen, an' let him sleep in the storeroom," Pardee said promptly.

Cheyenne was the heavy-set man who had been holding a gun in Ran's back. Now he led the way back along a hall into the kitchen. Beans, meat, and a stack of tortillas were on a table.

Ran had just filled a tin plate when Pardee came in and filled a second one. "Got to feed beauty," he said, grinning as he went out.

Cheyenne watched Ran attack the food. "My God!" he exclaimed. "No man could be that hungry!"

"You're findin' out." Ran smiled. "How about gettin' me a belt an' gun?"

"Pardee'll have to do that. You won't need a gun to-night."

"Guess not. What's on Pardee's mind?"

"He'll have to tell you that, too."

Ran asked no more questions. When the plate was empty, he sighed with satisfaction, rolled a cigarette, asked for his bed.

Cheyenne unlocked a door at the end of the kitchen, revealing a small, dark room.

"The Mex' cook's in there," he stated. "Kick him outta his blanket an' make yourself comfortable."

The storeroom was filled with barrels, sacks, boxes. The

walls were lined with shelves. Two windows, high up, were too small for a man to get through. On the floor lay a snoring figure rolled in a blanket.

Cheyenne closed the door. A key turned in the lock. Ran smiled wryly to himself in the blackness. They weren't taking any chances on his leaving in the night. Ignoring the Mexican cook, he lay down on the floor. In two minutes he was sound asleep.

A hand on his shoulder awoke Ran in the morning. "Time to roll out," Cheyenne said.

The kitchen was fragrant with breakfast. Two frightened-looking Mexican women were helping the morose cook. An armed guard sat in a chair. Ran went out to the pump, stripped to the waist, and washed.

He felt better as he pulled on his shirt and looked around. People had ranched here a long time, he decided. Men had planted those great cottonwoods long years back. The valley looked fresh and smiling in contrast to the harsh Por Nada. In all directions were low hills. Faintly visible, off in the south through the misty blue distance, were the peaks of higher mountains.

Those peaks must be in old Mexico. Ran was thoughtful as he turned back into the house. He noticed Cheyenne leaning in the open doorway, watching him. Pardee must still be suspicious.

Breakfast was eaten in the dining room off the opposite end of the kitchen. The bright sun sifted through gay curtains. Anne Kilpatrick's touch was visible everywhere.

Pardee was surly. He wolfed the food an uneasy Mexican woman set before him and said little until he finished and rolled a cigarette. Then he turned to Ran.

"I reckon we can use you, Malone . . . even if the girl did

bring you in like a whipped pup. There's plenty of fight ahead . . . an' plenty of money afterward."

"Right now," said Ran, "I'd rather have a gun. I don't feel dressed without one."

"You'll get a gun."

"Uhn-huh. Where's all this money you aim to get?"

"The Kilpatricks," Pardee said curtly, "own a mine a couple of hundred miles south of the border. The oldest brother runs it. Hell is popping from Mexico City to Nogales these days. Old General José Lazaro is on the prod in the north. He's raided the mine a couple of times . . . but he didn't get it all, not by a damned sight."

Pardee drained his coffee cup and set it down hard in the thick saucer.

"Lazaro had sense enough not to stop the mine. It's a fat goose that'll lay an egg whenever he needs it. But they haven't been able to ship out any metal. It's been pilin' up there, hid away. But Lazaro can get it whenever he makes up his mind. He's got ways of makin' folks talk."

Pardee grinned at the thought. Leaning his elbows on the table, he inhaled deeply and continued with smoke dribbling from his mouth.

"Kilpatrick decided to try slipping his gold across the border secretly. He sent out a shipment in a wagon an' got it through. He's ready to make a big play an' get everything out he can. It's comin' here to the ranch. He'll have every gun he can trust along to guard it, and he'll have charge of it hisself. We'll get it here," said Pardee, grinning.

"How'd you find out all this?" Ran asked carefully.

" 'Lonzo Jones, there acrost from you, worked at the mine as a guard. He seen the first shipment go out an' heard 'em plannin' for the big one. 'Lonzo figgered he'd never get rich packin' a gun there at the mine. He quit and hightailed it to Globe, where I was. 'Lonzo an' me has done business before. I had some of the boys with me an' I knew where to get word to the rest. We scattered an' headed this way to take the ranch. All we got to do is sit tight here. Last night just before you got here a Mex' rode in to say Harry Kilpatrick'd be in tomorrow or next day from the mine. Are you ready to make the fight with us?"

Pardee had planned well. He always did, and, in spite of himself, Ran's pulse beat faster at the thought of the stakes. Bar gold! Loot from a rich mine! Any man's gold who could take it and hold it! Men on the outlaw trail dreamed about such a chance and seldom got it. The score with Pardee could be put off for a time. Those outlaw years back in the Nueces country had hardened Ran. Many things he would not do—but man against man, gun against gun, keen wits on both sides, made a fair gamble.

"I'll side with the rest of you," Ran told Pardee.

During the morning two Mexican cowhands rode in unsuspectingly. They were disarmed and locked up with the rest of the hands in the adobe bunkhouse. Two men had been killed when the ranch had been taken over; eight now were locked in the bunkhouse. Two of Pardee's men stood constant guard outside.

The horses were in the corrals, eating well, resting. No roads ran near the ranch. Travelers seldom came this way. The lay-out was perfect.

Anne Kilpatrick and her brother came out for exercise, guarded by two armed men. Ran was leaning against the back of the house, smoking a cigarette, when they came by. She had been on his mind in a vague, disquieting way. Now Ran straightened, searching her face.

Much of her weariness had vanished. She had washed,

donned clean clothes, fixed her hair. But no girl could go through what she had stood and not bear signs of it.

Anne Kilpatrick's face was still wan; purple shadows lay under her eyes. They made her look prettier, Ran thought. Chin up, still stubborn, proud, showing no traces of fear, she looked smaller than ever this morning. She stopped before him, coldly antagonistic.

"So you *are* one of them, after all? Everything you said was a lie."

The young man beside her had a bloody bandage about one arm. He was a shade taller than Ran, perhaps a year or so older; his tanned face bore a certain likeness to Anne Kilpatrick's. In common they had that stubborn, unbeaten air.

Cold gray eyes met Ran's look. "So this is the one who shot Johnny Black in the back?" Bill said to his sister.

The two guards stood behind them, grinning at the diversion. Ran ignored them and eyed the Kilpatricks, brother and sister.

"I happened to be tellin' the truth," he said calmly. "I never saw this Johnny Black. Wouldn't have shot him in the back if I had. I don't handle my guns that way."

"No?" said Anne Kilpatrick with her little chin up. "We know why you men are here." Color rushed into her cheeks; her voice grew stormy. "If anything happens to my brother Harry, I'll do my best to see that the last one of you. . . ."

"Stop it, Anne!" her brother broke in curtly. "You're wasting breath. Mister," he said to Ran, "Johnny Black was an old friend of mine. I won't forget the man who shot him in the back."

One of the guards chuckled, broke in. "If Pardee has his way, mebbe you won't remember it long, either. Me, now, I don't see why he don't shoot the lot of you an' get it over with."

Grinning, the other one said: "I reckon Pardee's got a soft spot in his heart fer a purty face. Business before pleasure . . . but I ain't ever heard of him passin' up any pleasure."

"Come on, Anne," Bill Kilpatrick said stonily.

The girl's face was pale as she went on with him. But it seemed to Ran that her eyes were unseeing as they stared ahead, or perhaps they were seeing, picturing visions that made the ride across the Por Nada seem a pleasure trip.

That blindly staring look stayed with Ran. He told himself irritably nothing was wrong with her—yet. And her business was none of his business. Only the gold—and Black Pardee—were his business.

That night Ran slept on the living room floor with three of the other men. Morning brought a growing air of expectancy. Today, if everything went well, the gold from the Kilpatrick mine would be in. Pardee was almost jovial. Extra ammunition was brought out. Guns were inspected, cleaned, tried out.

Pardee himself gave Ran two cartridge belts, two revolvers, a Winchester rifle, and a hunting knife.

"Better get used to your guns," he said significantly. "You'll need 'em plenty when the time comes."

Fresh blood was caked on one of the cartridge belts. "I hope his luck ain't comin' to me with this," Ran said, smiling faintly as he indicated the blood.

"You're makin' your own luck," Pardee told him bluntly.

By now Ran knew that Anne Kilpatrick and her brother were locked in one of the bedrooms. For some reason Pardee was showing them extra consideration, although the man who guarded the front of the house looked in the window every time he passed, and there was always someone inside the house near their door.

The sun was hot. The man on guard went inside now and then for water. Ran came to the window at a time when the guard was inside. Rolling a cigarette, he stopped and spoke without looking inside.

"Miss Kilpatrick."

She was there a moment later, regarding him distrustfully. The purple shadows were deeper under her eyes. She looked as if she had not slept much during the night.

"I just wanted to tell you not to worry about what might happen to you," Ran told her.

"I don't understand."

"Don't try, but don't worry about Pardee."

Bitterly she said: "Are you offering to protect me?"

"If you need it," Ran said shortly.

"Does that include my brother?"

"Nope," said Ran. "He's a man. He'll have to take his chances."

"I see," Anne Kilpatrick said coldly. Her voice grew stormy again, scornful, bitter. "Do you think I'd believe you? I'd sooner trust a rattler! I'd take the word of the worst Mexican *ladrón* south of the border before yours!"

"Wait a minute, Anne!" Bill Kilpatrick urged, appearing beside her. "This man didn't prove so dangerous on the way here."

"He didn't have a chance!"

"If he's any good at all, he did have a chance from what you've told me about it." Bill Kilpatrick's face had taken on lines over night. "Malone," he said bluntly through the window, "I'm worried about my sister. Why do you want to help her?"

Ran grinned faintly. "I never knew I was as bad as a rattler or a Mexican *ladrón*. Maybe I am . . . but I don't fight women or see 'em hurt. That's all."

"Will you take word to my brother?" Kilpatrick asked cautiously. "I'll make it worth your while."

"Damn you, no!" Ran retorted. "I reckon you listened too hard to your sister then! You oughta know better than to ask that."

Pardee walked off the front porch just then and saw Ran standing before the window. He scowled and started toward the spot.

"What's the idea of hangin' around that window, Malone?" he called.

Ran walked to meet him, drawing deliberately on the cigarette. "I was talkin' to them, Pardee."

"Talkin'? By God, what's the idea?" Pardee grated, halting before him.

"Any reason why I shouldn't? You want the window watched while your man's inside, don't you?"

"What've you got to talk to them about, Malone?"

"I was tryin' to find out what the jasper looked like who shot their foreman." Ran grinned.

Pardee swore. "Never mind about that! Keep away from them!"

Still grinning, Ran spoke softly: "Don't tromp on me, Pardee. I'm with you on this little gold *pasear* . . . but I'm still Ran Malone. I don't take kindly to bein' cussed out, unless the gent is smilin'."

"You're getting damned independent, Malone!"

"Hell, Pardee, I've been that way all along. Don't get your ropes crossed."

Scowling, Pardee started to answer that, then spat and gritted: "I'm tellin' you to keep away from them if you want to stay healthy! I never did warm to you, Malone! I took you on here because we're gonna need all the gun work we can scrape up! But I'm givin' orders around here an' I'll make it hot for the man who crosses me!"

At midday the truth of that was borne in on Ran with unexpected suddenness. Most of them were at the table eating dinner when two quick shots from the men standing guard out in front brought them away from the table with a rush. As they burst out of the front door, led by Black Pardee, Ran saw the guard running toward a staggering figure that had come up from the creekbank past the tall cottonwoods.

Ran swore silently to himself. Only one man could be walking in like that from the direction of the Por Nada. The man they had left at Yaqui Pool had come afoot here to the Kilpatrick ranch, to Black Pardee and his men.

V

As he ran with the others, Ran furiously felt he should have thought of this, should have planned for it, but now it was too late. There was nothing to do but face it.

"My God, it's Bull Carson! He must 'a' lost his horse!" one of the men yelled.

Carson could still stand as they gathered around him. He had gotten water back there along the creek, of course, but he was in bad shape. He had lost pounds of weight and looked more dead than alive. Pardee fired the first question as Ran came within earshot.

"What happened to you, Bull? I figured you wasn't comin'."

Carson started to answer, then his glance stopped on Ran. A stream of curses came from him. "There's the dirty son-of-a-bitch that stole my hoss and put me afoot!" he raved. "Him and that damned girl! Gimme your gun, Pardee! I'll kill him!"

Carson tore Pardee's gun from his holster as he spoke. Ran flipped one of his guns out as Pardee grabbed Carson's hand and shouted: "Hold on! No shootin'!"

A man caught Ran's arm from behind. Another man got the other arm. Carson, wild with fury, struggled until Pardee tore the gun away from him.

"What the hell's all this?" Pardee exploded, glaring from one to the other of them. "Carson, are you sayin' Malone put you afoot?"

"I don't know what'n hell his name is, but that's the one!" Carson panted, thrusting his arm at Ran. "They put me afoot at Yaqui Pool! Took my guns an' hoss!"

Scowling, Pardee addressed Ran. "You didn't say anything about it, Malone."

"No reason why I should. It wasn't any of your business, Pardee."

"The Kilpatrick girl brought you in here a prisoner. How come you helped her put Bull afoot? What was the idea?"

Carson cursed thickly. "He was tied up when they hit Yaqui Pool . . . but she cut him loose an' they rode off together plenty sociable!"

Pardee ripped out an oath. "You told me that was your hoss, Malone! You said you rode him into the Por Nada, leadin' the other hoss! You lied to me, Malone! What for?"

"I don't like being questioned, Pardee."

"You don't?" said Black Pardee. His eyes were narrowed now. He was thinking hard. "If you lied about Bull's hoss, you lied about the rest of it! By God, Malone, you knew who you was followin' into the Por Nada! An' you kept a-comin' . . . lookin' fer him!"

"I was brought in to be turned over to the sheriff," Ran reminded. "How could I know who'd be here?"

But Pardee's rage was rising. "You followed *me* here!" he charged angrily. "When you found the girl afoot, you brought her along, too! You always was soft-hearted like that, Malone! But you kept a-comin' . . . after me! When you got a chance to get Bull's hoss, you took it! You been tryin' to trick me, Malone! Get his guns, boys! I'll fix the skunk!"

Jumping back, Ran broke the hold on his right arm. The other man held tightly to the left arm. Ran's right hand streaked for his gun. Before he could draw it, he was pistol slugged from behind.

His knees buckled. He went down, and his last memory was of booted feet kicking him.

Ran came out of it to find log ceiling *vigas* overhead. He was on his back, looking up at them. He hurt all over. The pain which had been in his head before was mild compared to the hurt there now. He turned his head as a low voice said: "I guess he'll be all right now."

Ran saw he was in the bedroom. Anne Kilpatrick and her brother were standing beside the bed. No particular sympathy was visible on their faces, but the girl's bitter animosity was not there, either.

Ran tried to sit up. Kilpatrick helped him. The bedspread and pillow were splotched with blood. Ran's shirt was bloody, too.

He was groggy, sore all over, but he found that he could stand. A mirror hanging over a handmade chest of drawers caught his eye. Stepping to it, Ran peered at a face that hardly resembled the one he was used to. They had given him the "boot", had kicked and trampled him unmercifully.

176

Anne Kilpatrick and her brother were watching him when he turned from the mirror. Ran forced a grin. It hurt.

"The man we met at Yaqui Pool walked here," Ran said to her. "He was one of Pardee's men."

"I don't see why that should have made any difference," she said gravely.

"It did. When Pardee found I'd covered up a little on how I got here, it started him thinkin'. He began to wonder what I was doin' in the Por Nada . . . an' he didn't like the answer."

"What *were* you doing in the Por Nada?" Anne Kilpatrick questioned.

Ran chuckled ruefully. "Not shootin' your foreman in the back. I was followin' the man who did it."

"This man Pardee?" she guessed. "Why didn't I think about it before? He's wearing bat-wing chaps, also."

"You'll never prove it in a law court, so why figure? Fact is, there ain't much chance of gettin' Pardee into any court."

"One outlaw following another outlaw," the girl said. "He did something to you."

Ran grinned at her, but said nothing.

Kilpatrick said: "Malone, what do you intend to do?"

"Get outta here an' save my skin if I can," Ran said violently. "I've had enough!"

"I suppose you *would* feel that way," Anne remarked coldly.

Kilpatrick was looking slightly disgusted with himself as Ran limped to the window and looked out. Cheyenne was standing out there, smoking.

"You must be made outta mule hide an' jerky," Cheyenne declared. "Damned if I thought you'd get up again after Pardee got through with you."

"What's on his mind now?" Ran asked.

Cheyenne shrugged. "I'd hate to be in your shoes, Malone. Pardee told the boys to lock you up an' he'd take care of you later. Whatever you done to Pardee, it must 'a' been bad to set him off thataway. Like a crazy man, he was."

"It ain't the first time he's been crazy," Ran said curtly. "He's got a yellow streak as wide as the horns on a Sonora steer. It makes him twice as mean when he's got the upper hand."

"Yellah? Hell, you're crazy, Malone!"

"Pardee can't stand a knife," Ran said. "He never goes without a gun, if he can help it. An' he always carries a Derringer in case he's cornered."

"Where'd you get all that?"

"I ran the same range long enough to know his sign."

Cheyenne spat. "Too bad it won't help you now. Pardee's out on his hoss. When he comes back, I reckon he'll sling his loop for you."

"And none of you rannies'll see I get a man's chance."

"Hell! We're here after gold, Malone. If Pardee's got a feud to settle with you, that's his business."

"I figured so," Ran said mildly. He stood there at the window as Cheyenne walked on.

Then Bill Kilpatrick joined him. "Easy enough to get out this window and make a run for it, Malone," he suggested.

"An' get a bullet in your back *pronto*." Ran shrugged. "The horses are guarded. There's no cover. It wouldn't even be sport to stop you."

"I'll be all right, if you want to try it, Bill," Anne said suddenly.

"You remind me of a rabbit showin' its teeth at a curly wolf." Ran grinned. He saw some cut lengths of rope in a corner and picked them up. "Anybody been tied with these?"

"Both of us, at night," Bill Kilpatrick answered grimly.

The longest piece of rope was about nine feet. Ran sat down on the bed and made a running noose in one end.

"No use," Bill Kilpatrick said, watching him. "They come in that door with their guns out, ready for trouble."

"Might hang one of us from a *viga* with it," Ran said amiably. "Either one of you got a knife hidden away?"

They hadn't.

"What would you do with a knife?" Anne Kilpatrick questioned alertly.

"That," Ran chuckled, "is somethin' that always comes in handy. I know a man who carried one down the back of his neck. Wish I'd got the habit."

He rolled a cigarette and smoked thoughtfully. A rib felt broken; his left arm was strained at the shoulder; a hip had been kicked until the joint seemed to be cracked. All that from Pardee, who could kick a man to death, and had, who would shoot a man in the back, leave a woman alone in a place like the Por Nada. The gold didn't seem so important when you got to thinking about that.

The sun had set when Pardee and a companion galloped to the front of the house. A prisoner rode between them on a travel-stained horse.

Swinging down, Pardee spoke loudly to the men who came out to meet them. "Kilpatrick sent this chicken ahead to say they'd be coming on YK land through the Notch about midnight. Kilpatrick wants a fresh team for his wagon. His hosses are givin' out."

"Where's the Notch?" the nearest man asked.

"About twelve miles out. If someone don't meet 'em

there, they'll be suspicious." Pardee smiled as he hitched up his gun belt. His rasping chuckle carried to the window where Ran was listening. "We'll meet 'em, all right, boys. This *hombre* says they've got eight men with guns. It'll be easy."

Behind Ran, Bill Kilpatrick groaned softly. "The Notch is a perfect place for an ambush. Harry and his men won't have a chance."

"How do you get there?" Ran asked.

VI

Pardee and his men were eating in the other part of the house as darkness fell. Three plates of food were brought into the bedroom. Cheyenne waited in the doorway with a drawn gun while the Mexican woman set the plates down, cast a look of frightened pleading at Anne Kilpatrick and her brother.

Ran spoke to Cheyenne. "Are you doin' all Pardee's dirty work?"

"He knows I'll dump you cold an' quick if there's any funny business," Cheyenne retorted, backing out, closing and locking the door.

There had been activity at the corrals. One of the men had ridden off with a harness team on lead ropes. Ran hurriedly ate some of his food, blew out the lamp, and stepped to the window.

A faint star glow had replaced the last light of day. In the dead silence that fell over the bedroom, the voices of the men could be heard in the dining room and, nearer, the steps of the guard out in front scraped softly on the ground.

The man came to the open window, stopped before it, and spoke suspiciously, "What's the matter with the lamp in there?"

"It went out," Ran said.

"Light it again."

"We're out of matches."

"Here's a couple." The man stepped close to the window and put them on the ledge.

He couldn't see into the room; he suspected nothing until the running noose flicked out and around his head. Then it was too late. Ran's weight on the nine-foot length of rope jerked the strangling head clear over the window sill. The guard's yell choked off at his lips. Instead of fighting the noose, he pulled his gun and fired two shots into the room. Then Bill Kilpatrick reached the window, grabbed the gun, wrenched it away, and slugged at the head.

"Damn him! They'll be outside quick now!" Ran snapped, letting the limp figure slide back to the ground. "You want to try it?"

"Can't!" Bill Kilpatrick said, shoving the gun into Ran's hand. "He put a bullet in my leg! Take Anne!"

Anne Kilpatrick said fiercely: "I won't leave you, Bill!"

Ran was already going through the window. "Here they come!" he snapped. "Too late now! So long!"

He sprawled heavily over the unconscious guard, scrambled up as the front door was kicked open and men ran out.

"What's the matter, Red?" the first man yelled.

Ran stooped, fumbled for the buckle of the guard's gun belt. He wanted those cartridges. But the man had fallen face down on it. He was limp, heavy—and three men were off the porch now, turning toward him, and more coming.

Ran took a knife, left the belt there, and slipped back

along the house wall. Their eyes would not be used to the darkness for a moment yet. One of the men, running toward the window, stumbled over the guard before Ran could reach the corner of the long house. He saw Ran.

"There's one of them!" he shouted.

Bullets were smashing closely as Ran dove around the corner of the house to brief safety. They were following him. He made the back corner of the house, cut over toward the corral, and too late realized that the horses were saddled and hitched at the back of the house.

The shots had stopped. Pardee's voice bawled orders. "Watch the hosses! Fork leather an' ride him down!"

Three cartridges were in the revolver Ran clutched in his sweating hand, perhaps four cartridges, if the man had been reckless enough to carry a full cylinder. Four bullets would do little good if Pardee's men came throwing lead. Crouching, Ran raced toward the corrals.

They knew the general direction he took. After that, they sought him blindly. Their comments made that plain.

"Which way'd he go?"

"I didn't see him."

The corrals were empty. Hoofs beat hard as riders spurred out that way. Ran rolled under the bottom pole of the first corral and hugged the ground. Men rode within twenty feet. They combed and quartered all about, gradually working away. Pardee's furious voice floated back.

One man stayed by the bunkhouse, riding slowly back and forth. Ran considered the chance of shooting him out of the saddle and getting the horse. But if he missed, if the man got away, he'd be afoot, with the rest knowing where he was.

So, leaving the corral, Ran slipped toward the creek

bank. Two men only had gone this way. Neither came close. Ran waded the creek, climbed the low bank, and broke into a trot, heading south.

Half an hour later the ranch buildings were out of sight and sound. Ran stopped in the sandy bed of an arroyo, built a cigarette, sat down while he considered. He had hoped for a horse, and there was no chance now of getting one. His hip was no better; his side hurt worse. A lifetime in the saddle had not helped him as a walker. But when the cigarette burned low, Ran headed for the nearest rise of ground, took his bearings, and set off in a fast, limping walk.

An hour later, following Bill Kilpatrick's directions, he struck the wagon trail to the Notch. Straight enough until it reached the first hills, the road became rough, winding, up and down. It made hard going for high-heeled riding boots, for a man not used to walking.

The rising moon drowned starlight with silvery brilliance, but rocks, bushes, stunted trees offered cover now. Horses came up from behind at a steady trot. Ran left the road. He was crouching behind a small bush when Black Pardee and his men rode by. Plain in the moonlight, they rode grimly, silently, with intent purpose understandable when you knew what they were riding for.

Anne Kilpatrick, along with her brother, was riding in their midst, head up, face stonily forward—Anne Kilpatrick, riding to that bloody gunfight with them—and there was nothing a man on foot with only three bullets could do about it. Ran watched her out of sight, and, before the sound of their passing had died away, he was limping after them, bleak-faced, cold, and grim.

The Notch cut through a rocky ridge on the southeast of the ranch. Miles away, from the crest of a ridge, Ran saw the V-shaped Notch under the moon. That was the only point for a long distance where a wagon could get through from the border.

Bill Kilpatrick had described it harshly: "It isn't wide. The sides are rocky. A hundred men could hide there, night or day, and wipe anyone coming through. Harry and his men won't have much chance if they're surprised in there."

Ran had no watch, but the moon rose steadily as the hours passed. Blisters on his feet broke, and the raw flesh was rubbed sore. Muscles ached; pain grew worse. Now and then he swore at himself for being a fool. He still wasn't clear as to what he was going to do, or why. He had wanted some of that gold in fair fight, and now he found himself wanting something else still more. He wanted Anne Kilpatrick to look at him without bitter scorn—but above all he wanted Pardee.

As he neared the rocky ridge, Ran began to listen for shots. It was about midnight. Coyotes were yapping again; now and then a rabbit scurried away. But the landscape appeared deserted, peaceful.

Half a mile before the grade started up, Ran struck off across the rough open toward the base of the steep ridge. Soon he was climbing, gasping for breath. Sweating, growing weak from pain and the struggle up over the rocks, Ran finally made the top and stood gulping great breaths. On both sides of the ridge the country stretched away into pale, silver distance. The crest was not wide. Walking across it, Ran looked across a flat valley to a higher barrier of hills, and down there on the plain, a mile or so away, a pinpoint of light flared, died. A match had been lighted and tossed away. That would be the Kilpatrick men coming to the Notch—and to Pardee.

Making no noise, Ran walked along the crest to the edge of the Notch. Black shadows started part way down and filled the bottom. Dirt had washed off the side slopes, leaving rocky ledges, rocks of all sizes. Ran started down warily, keeping low and testing each foothold before he put weight on it.

At the west end of the Notch a horse whinnied softly, another stamped. But Pardee's men made no sound. The grind of steel-tired wheels approached on the grade leading up into the Notch. Men galloped on ahead of the wagon. One of them helloed loudly. One of Pardee's men yelled back. Ran's foot dislodged a small stone. It rolled for many feet, striking rock after rock. Pardee's annoyed voice floated up.

"Who did that? Who's up there?"

"Hell! You know we're all down here, Pardee!" one of the men replied.

The riders coming on ahead of the gold-laden wagon were just entering the Notch. Ran fired two shots down the slope toward the last speaker.

VII

Pardee's enraged yell joined the echoes. "That's Malone, damn him. He's up there!"

Ran answered: "You're right. Pardee! I've come for you! Come with a knife! I reckon you know why!"

The wagon had halted. The Kilpatrick men rode quickly into the rocks beside the road. A hail came from them.

"Who's that? What's wrong?"

"Nine men waitin' - to bushwhack your gold!" Ran shouted.

"Damn you, Malone! I'll kill you for this!" Pardee

185

bawled from below. "You men with the wagon! Where's Harry Kilpatrick?"

"I'm here. What is it?" a curt voice replied.

"We've got your sister an' brother, Kilpatrick! If you want 'em alive, throw down your guns! Leave your hosses there an' walk off from the wagon!"

Anne Kilpatrick's clear voice cried out: "Don't do it, Harry! They'll kill. . . ." She broke off, crying out in pain.

Ran heard a brief scuffle. Bill Kilpatrick cried: "I'll get you for that!" Then Pardee grated: "I guess that'll hold you!" Bill Kilpatrick did not speak again.

"Cheyenne!" Pardee called. "Take Smiley an' get Malone! The rest of you shoot them Kilpatrick men outta the rocks!"

Ran lifted his voice again. "Don't hurt the girl, Pardee, or I'll put a knife in your throat!"

"Damn you. Cheyenne, get him!"

That was Pardee's fear of cold steel speaking. An instant later two guns opened fire up the slope toward Ran. As if it were a signal for the taut, waiting men, hell broke loose below. Both sides opened fire. Anne Kilpatrick was down there in the thick of it.

Bullets smashed on the rocks close to Ran, as, on his stomach, he wriggled half a dozen yards down the slope to the shelter of a big boulder. Cheyenne and Smiley weren't sure where he was. Their bullets continued to strike higher up the slope, but as he dodged to the next bit of cover, one of them saw him. A bullet struck closely and ricocheted shrilly past his head.

One man was coming up the hill toward Ran. The flash from his gun muzzle was in a different spot this time, but he was shooting at shadows. Ran was wriggling down the slope to the shadow line, wondering where the second man was.

186

More Kilpatrick men had joined the first ones. They seemed to realize it was better to make a stand here among the rocks than to retreat into the open with the heavy wagon. Of Anne Kilpatrick there was no further sign. Not thirty yards away a gun flashed again as a man made his way stubbornly up the slope where he imagined Ran to be. Then, as Ran watched that spot for an instant, a gun roared just below him, where the second man had been waiting.

The bullet struck Ran in the left arm. He fell flat, and a second shot grazed his back.

The man up the hillside shouted: "Didja get him, Cheyenne?"

With hoarse satisfaction, Cheyenne replied: "I reckon so! Knocked him over like a long-eared jack!"

Gritting his teeth from the pain, Ran thumbed back the hammer of his gun and waited. The battle below drowned out Cheyenne's movements, but, lifting his eyes to the top of the small rock that served as shelter, Ran saw a dark blot coming to him. It hurt to put his weight on his wounded arm, but he held himself steady that way and fired his last shot carefully. The dark figure dropped, lay there.

Cheyenne was floundering weakly when Ran got to him. He tried to lift his gun and shoot. Ran stamped it to the ground, tore it out of the weak grip.

"I hope you fry in hell fer this!" Cheyenne gasped as Ran took his gun belt.

"I'll see you there then," Ran retorted. He was lying on the ground as he spoke, dodging shots from the other man. Cheyenne's rifle was there, also. Ran took it and scrambled for the shelter of the nearest big rock. There he strapped on the belt, reloading both handguns. Blood was streaming down his left arm. Movement hurt the arm—but he could use it stiffly.

The man named Smiley was still stalking him, but cautiously now. From this point down to the road the shadows grew blacker. Ran took a chance, went down in a dodging rush, and lost himself in the rocks near the road. Pardee's men had worked nearer the other end of the Notch, to get opposite the Kilpatrick men. Ran went that way, too. Down here where the moonlight did not strike, you had to be on a man before you knew who he was.

Picking the nearest gun flash, Ran stalked the man, coming up behind him. He waited a moment for another shot, and then closed in. The man heard him at the last moment and turned, calling: "Who is it?"

Ran clubbed him to the ground with a gun barrel and went on without stopping, for that man was not Pardee. The Kilpatrick guns seemed to be slackening off, but a bullet, clipping Ran's leg, made him realize that Kilpatrick lead might also drop him. It did not matter much. Blood was all over his left arm—and he had to find Pardee. He dropped another man the same way, and still another man.

Pardee's bawling voice suddenly rang out. "Hold on everybody!"

The Pardee men ceased firing. The Kilpatrick men followed. Everyone could hear Pardee's harsh voice.

"Cheyenne! Where's Malone?"

There was no answer.

Harry Kilpatrick called across the road: "Anne! Where are you?"

She answered, and Ran swallowed a lump in his throat at what she said.

"He hasn't shot me yet, Harry! Don't mind me!"

Pardee called out harshly. "We're comin' across the road, Kilpatrick! Your sister'll be in front. If you want to shoot, she'll get it! An' if you drop one of us, I'll put a bullet in her myself! Boys, get close around me!"

You could almost hear Harry Kilpatrick groan aloud. He did the only thing he could. "Let 'em come, men!" he ordered.

"Harry, don't be a fool!" Anne Kirkpatrick cried. She was with Pardee, some thirty yards ahead.

Pardee's men began to close in on that spot, and Ran moved toward it, also. A death-like silence had fallen over the Notch, broken only by boots scraping on the rocks.

Then Pardee broke it: "Let's go, boys!"

They were a compact little group as they moved out across the road, but you had to be close to them to see it. Ran was just behind them. Pardee was in the middle, with Anne Kilpatrick walking in front of him. None of the men was behind Pardee. The why of that became clear in a muttered remark.

"This is a hell of a note, hidin' behind a woman's skirts!"

"Shut up, damn you!" Pardee flung at him. "You want that gold, don't you? They'll hold us here all night, an' have someone ridin' for help! You can thank that skunk, Malone, for this!"

Then they were across the road. Crowding close, Ran saw that Anne Kilpatrick's hands were tied behind her. Pardee was holding her wrists and carrying a belt gun in his other hand.

Ran shoved his extra gun inside his belt, drew the knife he'd taken off the man back at the ranch, dropped Cheyenne's rifle—and the next moment his weak left hand caught Pardee's neck and the knife blade was across the outlaw's throat.

"Get down!" Ran gritted softly. "Tell 'em to scatter out!"

Pardee went rigid. Breath whistled through his lips. A

faint gasp came from him as he carefully went down on his knees. He spoke thickly. "Boys . . . scatter out!"

"An' then what?" a voice asked.

"I'll . . . I'll tell you what to do."

"What's the matter? You sound funny," a man off to the left said.

"Damn you!" Pardee gasped. "Do what I say!"

He was down on his knees beside a huge rock. Anne Kilpatrick stood motionless. She had heard Ran's words, had turned her head, and now she stood silently.

Ran was in a cold sweat himself. His left arm was almost useless. His head was swimming with weakness. Pardee's men, almost within arm's reach, could kill all three with a storm of lead if they found they were being betrayed. They probably would, too, and it would give Ran small satisfaction to slit Pardee's throat if Anne Kilpatrick died at the same time.

"Anne," Ran whispered to her. "Know where your brother Harry is? Just ahead there?"

"Yes."

"Walk slowly to him. Tell him part of Pardee's men are gone. Then get down behind a rock an' stay there. You might," said Ran huskily, "say a prayer."

"And you?" said Anne Kirkpatrick.

"I'll be all right. Go on."

She went without speaking again, walking carefully off into the night. Only the *click* of her small riding boots on the stones came back.

"Pardee, what you doin'?" a man called.

Pardee shivered, remained mute as the sharp knife edge pressed harder against his throat. He would have charged, bellowing, into the muzzle of a gun, but cold steel left him a sweating wreck.

190

Danny Catron had found that out back in the Texas country, when Pardee had been pistol-whipping him for pure drunken pleasure. Danny Catron had drawn his only weapon, a knife, and Pardee had bolted out of the room before he remembered he had a gun in his hand. Within a month Danny Catron had been shot in the back. A Mexican goat herder had seen Pardee riding the same road half an hour earlier.

Pardee had been out of the Nueces country by the time Ran got back from Fort Worth. That might have been the end of it, except that Danny Catron had left a widow and three young children, and Danny Catron had been Ran Malone's best friend, although one was an outlaw and one an honest homesteader.

Now Pardee knelt with cold steel against his throat while the long seconds dragged. To the kneeling man Ran husked softly: "You haven't forgotten Danny Catron, Pardee? He told me how you liked a knife. Danny'd like to see me cut your throat tonight. I followed you a long time, Pardee. For a little I figured I could get some of the gold for Danny's widow. But I reckon now all I can do is send you to hell after Danny!"

Pardee shuddered. The ghost of a whimper oozed from him. "Gimme a chance, Malone!"

"Like the chance you gave Danny Catron?"

Pardee's men were growing restless. "For Gawd's sake, what's the matter with you, Pardee?" one of them burst out in exasperation.

Low voices drifted from the rocks where the Kilpatrick men were hidden. Suddenly Harry Kilpatrick called: "Malone! Watch yourself! We're comin' to clean out what's left of those skunks!"

Pardee had dropped his gun. Ran kicked it aside with his

foot and dropped down behind Pardee as the Kilpatrick men started forward, firing as they came. They came with a rush, confident, irresistible. Pardee's men held their ground only for a moment—then they broke, scrambling back among the rocks, firing only to cover their retreat.

The wave of battle rolled past the spot where Ran and his prisoner crouched. A man turned aside, calling: "Malone!" It was Harry Kilpatrick.

"Here!" Ran said. "Here's your man."

When Harry Kilpatrick stood before them, Ran stood up, taking his knife from Pardee's throat, letting Pardee stand up.

"Man!" said Harry Kirkpatrick huskily, oblivious to the lead still flying. "You don't know what you've done for me! Anne says Bill is only knocked unconscious across the road there. But if anything had happened to her, why . . . why. . . ."

Pardee had stood up slowly. Kilpatrick was still fumbling for words to show his gratitude when Pardee's arm made a sudden movement, twisting, as if to shake something down out of his sleeve.

The knife in Ran's hand flashed like the strike of a snake's head. The keen blade entered Pardee's neck from the side, and, as Pardee reeled aside, the Derringer he had shaken out of his sleeve went off with a loud report. He fell heavily, with the knife still in his neck, and kicked convulsively on the ground.

"I came a long way to get him," Ran said. "I'm kinda glad it was this way, the way he was most afraid of. He couldn't face a knife."

"I understand you're an outlaw," Kilpatrick said bluntly.

"I am."

"You're only Malone here on the YK," said Harry Kilpatrick. "There's a heap I want to say to you later. I've got to catch up with my men now. Will you go back there and watch my sister?"

"If you think she'll be all right with me."

"She said she's never seen a man like you, Malone. She'll feel safe while you're with her."

They were still shooting down at the other end of the Notch, near the Pardee horses, but, as Ran Malone limped toward Anne Kilpatrick, he hardly heard the shots. For he knew that the bitter scorn had left her and that here in the Notch he had found gold worth more than the metal bars in that steel-tired wagon.

Reunion at Cottonwood Station

In 1950 T. T. Flynn, at the encouragement of his agent, Marguerite E. Harper, began writing book-length Western fiction. In this he proved extremely successful. Harper had a close working relationship with the editor of Dell Publishing's First Editions. These were original paperback novels, rather than reprints of hard cover books. Flynn's first novel, *The Man from Laramie* (Dell, 1954), was offered to *The Saturday Evening Post* where it was serialized in eight installments (1/2/54–2/20/54), for which the author was paid $40,000, and it was also sold to Columbia Pictures for the film version directed by Anthony Mann and starring James Stewart. Flynn's second novel, which was published first in paperback, was titled *Two Faces West* (Dell, 1954). It was made the basis for an eponymous television series— thirty-eight episodes broadcast beginning 10/17/60 and concluding 7/24/61, starring Charles Bateman in a dual rôle. Understandably Flynn stopped writing short stories, although he did produce two for Don Ward, editor of Dell Publishing's Western fiction magazines that, at the time, included the resurrected *All Western* and *Zane Grey's Western Magazine*. "Reunion at Cottonwood Station" was the first of the two and appeared in *All Western* (2–3/51).

Donovan got the letter in Tucson and took the first stage-coach to El Paso, and was standing in the gray clear twilight when the dusty passengers stepped out of the St. Louis stage.

Phil's whoop of delighted surprise hardly fitted a young graduate doctor, coming home to pills, pulses, and splinted bones. They pounded shoulders, shook hands, and stood grinning widely at each other.

"Had some business in El Paso," Donovan explained off-handedly.

Phil demanded: "What business?" His understanding grin made Donovan feel sheepish.

"Too many questions," Donovan growled. "Come on to the hotel and wash up, and get outside some steaks."

It had always been this way, more like brothers, Donovan had often thought, than father and son. In the hotel dining room they ate platter-size steaks and trimmings, and then strolled through the town, talking. On an impulse Donovan bought tickets to a shabby little theater near the Plaza, and a few minutes later, inside, Donovan's world fell in on him.

In the dim light, on the hard seat beside Phil, Donovan tasted nineteen years of silent bitterness, while the mother Phil could not remember moved there on the small bright stage, talking and laughing. Phil didn't know her, of course. On the badly printed program dodger, Vicky's name was Mrs. Blassingham. She'd been very young, really beautiful, Donovan had always thought. Now in the long-reaching noon of that beauty, Vicky was a little tired-looking, from whatever the years had brought her, and probably long disillusioned. But she was still Vicky, with the small mannerisms Donovan remembered so well, and the same laughter lilt in her tones.

Phil's enthusiastic whisper prodded: "Isn't she pretty?"

Donovan grudgingly muttered: "I suppose so." Then, startled, he looked at Phil.

"That black hair when the light strikes it," Phil whis-

195

pered his astounding discovery. "The way she moves . . . that smile!"

Vicky's hair was brown. Donovan had hardly noticed the black-haired girl. Unconscious relief sharpened the barb in his reply: "Since when did you start blathering about any filly who prances across a stage? Wake up!"

Phil gave him an uncertain look and fell silent. Half an hour later Donovan leaned to him in calm decision. "I should see Fred Kinsetter before we leave in the morning. Want you to meet him. Let's get going."

The girl was off stage, but Phil lingered briefly at the back of the dim hall before he reluctantly walked out with Donovan.

The second day after that, Donovan sat in the rear seat of the fast-rolling Tucson stage, covertly watching Phil's bemused expression, opposite him on the forward seat. *Still thinking of her,* Donovan thought with a twitch of annoyance. He glanced out the window when the steady run of the four horses changed to the confused trampling of a quickly reined halt. Brake blocks hit the dust-dripping wheel rims so hard the coach surged on its massive fore and aft straps.

Judge Elkins, a rotund, garrulous politician in the territory, slid half off the smooth leather seat and exclaimed: "Confound the man! What's he up to?"

The judge's spare, silent wife clung to the hand strap on her side, and Phil's look questioned. Donovan shrugged. The elegant Tucson sporting man beside Phil opened one eye, then tried to doze again. Young Second Lieutenant Tuckerman, traveling to his first command, stifled interest with another wrapping of military aloofness. Gray, thick dust sifted in, and Mrs. Elkins sneezed twice, thinly, like a kitten.

Phil said—*"Gesundheit!"*—and grinned at her.

She smiled back. Most people did to Phil, and it always pleased Donovan. Bill Leeds, the graying, experienced driver, had stepped down to the road. Donovan inquired out the window: "Anything wrong?"

"Seen somethin'," Leeds said briefly, and stalked to the rear.

Donovan stepped out to stretch, a medium-tall, vigorous man with a quality of solid purpose in his ruddy still-young face. He looked almost too young to be the father of Dr. Phil Donovan, and that pleased Donovan, too.

Back in the road, Leeds stooped and picked up an arrow. Donovan noted how the man straightened alertly and scanned the dry miles of semi-desert, patched with glossy-leaved greasewood, cacti, and low, bristling clumps of dark green bear grass.

When Donovan reached him, Leeds spoke briefly. " 'Pache arrow. Don't seem to be no blood on it."

Donovan reached for the fragile-looking shaft whose mere presence in the road dust had brought four galloping horses and a heavily loaded stage to a plunging halt. The iron-tipped point was sharp. Donovan thoughtfully touched it to a fingertip, and looked silently at Leeds.

"It never walked here," Leeds muttered, and took the arrow and stalked back past the stage.

Phil was at the step, black hat in hand, solid shoulders filling his well-tailored blue broadcloth. He topped Donovan by half an inch and was leaner and did not resemble Donovan closely. But they had the same dark, stubborn, driving eyes.

Donovan eyed Phil's thick shock of brown hair and thought: *A prime scalp.* Almost angrily he put the idea out of mind and explained: "He noticed that Apache arrow in the road."

Phil said—"Apache?"—and they heard Mrs. Elkins speak fretfully to the coach: "Why doesn't the man drive on?"

Donovan made a small gesture for Phil to come with him past the lathered, still-blowing horses, where Leeds had hurried. The Wells Fargo guard remained on the seat with a repeating rifle and was watching the landscape with restless intensity. Bill Leeds was moving slowly in the road, absently batting tiny dust puffs from a pants leg with the arrow shaft. He bent suddenly and came up with a pinch of road dirt. When they reached him, Leeds's resignation was almost sociable.

"Stage ahead of us passed here on the whip. See them hoof marks dug in?" Leeds gazed with shrewd, squinting eyes along the miles of road, dipping, rising, dipping. "Blood leaked from somethin' along here." He turned up a forefinger on which his callused thumb had mashed a small ball of still damp road dirt.

"Could I see that? I'm a doctor," Phil said mildly.

"He'p yourself, Doc. It ain't paint. A 'Pache arrow an' blood goes natural together." Leeds squinted again at the road ahead. "If Joe Kister made Cottonwood Station, we'll hear what happened." Bill Leeds's promise was soft and absent: "If Joe didn't make Cottonwood, we'll *see* what happened." Sober humor tugged a corner of his bleached mustache. "Joe was drivin' extra loaded with actor folks. I bet they never put on a show like they must 'a' seen along here."

Donovan watched Phil's quick interest, heard his question: "Were they the actors we saw in El Paso?"

"They come outta El Paso," said Leeds indifferently. His mind made up, he was almost curt. "All aboard, gents."

This, Donovan thought with foreboding, was suddenly a

day he would pay highly to wipe from reality. He should have inquired about the actors. The lashed horses surged into full gallop toward the Cottonwood relay station. Phil swayed on the lurching forward seat in frowning thought. All this was massive with irony that shook Donovan's complacency of years.

The stage rocked past a dead horse, its brass-studded collar still on the limp neck. Leeds shouted back to the windows: "If Kister had time to put out a hoss, he made Cottonwood!"

Donovan remembered Cottonwood Station. It was a lonely adobe building on a brush-choked flat. The station had a dug well and a lone cottonwood tree, and to the north was a line of yellow clay bluffs. A high adobe wall in back enclosed the tree, the well, and yard space. A man named Stofer kept the station, and his Mexican hostler had a timid wife and brood of chocolate-hued offspring.

The stage careened through bleach-bone sand of a dry channel and groaned up to level ground where the station stood. Stofer, a barrel-chested man, rifle in one hand, was signaling Leeds on around to the yard gate. A second man, rifle ready, watched in the open, and in the walled rear yard Donovan saw an old buckboard, two light ranch wagons, and the extra stagecoach.

Leeds hauled his foaming spans up beside the other coach. His soaring whoop let off the wire-hard strain of the last miles.

"Anyone need a doc? I got one!"

The noon sun was a metallic thrust on coach and wind-whistling spans and the hard-packed yard dirt on which Donovan stepped. The promise of howling slaughter all along the Tucson road was bottled in the hot walled yard by the slant of the heavy wooden gate.

Stofer hurried to the stage, blurting: "Who's the doc?"

"Here he is . . . Doctor Philip Donovan," said Donovan, and the full name was still a prideful relish on his tongue.

"Patchin' to do in there, Doc," Stofer said.

Phil was already reaching for the small leather satchel Leeds was handing down. He entered the station ahead of Stofer with a calm, convincing assurance Donovan hadn't noticed in him before. Donovan suspected much of it was new to Phil, too, and hiding uncertainties.

Kister, the driver of the extra stage, a short, energetic, profane man, was talking to Leeds. His words had the jumpy slap of recent reality.

"Five young bucks jumped us! On'y one had a rifle! But when they come up outta the scrub by the road, they sounded like blowed-up, blue-bellied hell was loose!"

Bill Leeds's elaborate yawn was a masterpiece of indifference. "Only five, Joe?"

Kister's indignation delighted every listening ear. "Hell's blazes! Could 'a' been a thousand behind 'em! They arrowed my wheeler an' shot a hole in my hat! Then they quirted ponies outta a gully an' chased us! There was arrows in the back boot till we looked like scalded porcupine huntin' home! I throwed a lucky shot into one, an' they broke it off! My wheeler give out a few miles on! Two passengers was wounded. You want it any closer'n that?"

"Me?" said Bill Leeds with vast disinterest. "Who said I wanted any of it?"

The laughter pushed back sober uncertainties that clotted in the yard. Donovan's inquiry sounded hardly interested: "What passengers were wounded?"

"Potbellied old gent got a bullet in his seat. An' a right pretty girl got a arrow graze on her right arm. If she hadn't leaned over just then, it'd spitted her like a Río Grande duck!"

"Would it be a Miss Senetra Boyd?"

"Somethin' like that."

This day, Donovan's foreboding prodded, kept stacking against him. Hurt slightly now, the black-haired girl would have Phil's utmost attention. Other news was not good. The eastbound stage had not come through. A ranch on Dry Creek, to the south, had been raided at daybreak. A Mexican boy had escaped through the brush to the next ranch with a warning, and those people, driving a light wagon furiously toward Cottonwood Station, had seen the dark smoke of their buildings blotching black on the horizon. West on the Tucson road two freighters had cut lead horses free, and in a running fight with six Apaches one man had managed to reach the station, wounded. On the yellow clay bluffs a long mile to the north, smoke signals had been rising. Young Lieutenant Tuckerman spoke his intensely loyal conviction: "The Army will quickly have all this in hand!"

"Gen'ral, you wave your army down when she comes through," Bill Leeds said tolerantly. "We got Joe Kister."

Donovan turned away from the fresh chuckles at Kister. Stofer was coming out of the station. Donovan stopped him.

"How are you for guns and cartridges?"

"Not good," said Stofer with bitter bluntness.

"And no help expected?"

Stofer's big hand flapped the idea away. He thumbed toward the doorway. "Hot grub in the kitchen. Whiskey. Be afternoon, I guess, before enough of them get together to try us, if that's what the smoke means."

The long front room of the station had whitewashed walls and peeled logs overhead. Donovan recalled it as a neat pleasant room, with a big pine table and hide chairs at one end, and a fireplace at the other end. Now women, children, and two men were in the long room, and a suppressed, tearing tension threaded the murmuring talk. Donovan's thoughts rode him darkly while he noted the small, deep-set front windows and the solid plank door, with heavy wooden bar leaning ready beside it.

He smiled at a solemn little girl with honey-colored braids and, when her doubtful smile came after a moment, he had an odd surge of pleasure. Then a bedroom door to the right of the fireplace opened and Mrs. Blassingham came out, and the wretched impact of dead years sledged Donovan.

She saw him and stopped, and her wide stare was a mute reach into the past. He moved toward her, and some great startled thought sent Vicky's look back into the room. Over her combed-back waves of brown hair, still soft-looking and fine, Donovan saw a narrow iron bed and a wounded man under a sheet smudged angry red in spots. Phil was washing hands in a tin basin on a small table. The black-haired girl was at Phil's elbow, holding a towel. She was tall, although Phil was taller, and she looked younger than Donovan had expected with straight black brows, a small gay nose, and merry mouth. They were smiling at each other.

Donovan's antagonism was a dark mood held in as Phil took the towel and glanced toward the doorway. Phil's smile widened.

"My first patient," he announced with unconscious pride. "And helping me as soon as her arm was re-bandaged. My father . . . Miss Senetra Boyd. And I see you and Missus Blassingham have met."

Donovan said calmly—"Yes."—and dipped his head courteously to the girl.

"I've told the ladies how we enjoyed their performance in El Paso."

202

"Yes," Donovan said. "Missus Blassingham, coffee was on my mind if you'd care for some."

Her intentness was all in the room, but she moved from the door to him, and Donovan's question was flat and distant. "Blassingham here?"

"The name is for convenience, Mark. I don't have a husband." And without looking at him: "Can we go outside and talk?"

A raw-boned man with a rifle, on guard out front, warned: "Ain't too safe out here."

"We'll watch," Donovan promised briefly, and the hot-coiled quiet of the brush-cluttered flats closed about their slow steps into the road.

Vicky's tone was wondering. "Mark, I didn't know him. You changed your name to Donovan."

"Yes," said Donovan evenly. "What happened to the man you went off with?"

"Another woman . . . very quickly. I came back, Mark, and you and Phil were gone."

Donovan nodded. "We pulled out, too. Phil was only three, but we managed."

"And married again?"

Donovan had two small cigars left in his leather case. He lighted one before replying. "God forbid. I had to hire help, of course."

Vicky's wondering tone reverted to Phil. "He didn't suspect who I was. Mark, what did you tell him?"

He had been braced for bitterness. Vicky had been volatile, impulsive with temper. This Vicky made him guardedly uncertain.

Reflectively Donovan said: "Phil heard only how good and beautiful his mother was. How she'd loved him."

Vicky's throat moved as she swallowed. "Thank you,

Mark, for that. Thank you."

Carefully Donovan said the rest of it. "Phil understands that his mother died of the fever when he was three. I don't think he'd take kindly to the truth about her now."

Vicky's slow steps followed the road edge. Her silence drew out. When Donovan suggested—"We'd better turn back."—she moved silently, not looking at him.

"You planned it, didn't you, Mark?" Vicky said finally. "You took him . . . all of him?"

Donovan could feel his pulse stepping up, and his first show of emotion graveled his tone. "That's right . . . all of him, Vicky! He's mine!"

Vicky's thread of reply finally came: "Mark, don't worry. You just evened everything between us." That was all. She was looking straight ahead.

Long ago Vicky's thoughts had baffled Donovan. They did now, and he used the same blunt coldness to cover it. "One thing you can do . . . keep that girl away from Phil."

Vicky's surprise studied him. "Why, Mark?"

"I want him to have his pick of the best."

The delayed slight smile that touched Vicky's mouth was not reassuring. "I approve of Senetra Boyd," she said calmly. Some belligerent challenge on Donovan's face must have sparked deep memories because Vicky then murmured—"Poor Mark."—and seemed to mean it. Gazing beyond the station, she asked: "Isn't that more Indian smoke?"

Donovan had been watching the new smoke erratically climbing above the yellow clay bluffs. "It is."

"Will they come here?"

"Probably." Donovan was watching the tall cottonwood behind the station. In the highest branches a brilliant beam of sunlight had lanced out. The Army sent messages that way, by heliograph, sunlight flashing from bright mirrors, and Second Lieutenant Tuckerman was just the fresh earnest young officer to think of it, and climb a tree.

"Mark!" Donovan looked at her, and Vicky said: "All these years, so many faces that weren't you or Phil. We're all three together now, for a few hours. Can't we make the best of it? A . . . a family reunion, in a way," she urged. "Only Phil won't know it, of course."

"What else can we do?" Donovan conceded warily. "But what about that girl?"

"Senetra," said Vicky calmly, "is your problem."

Donovan darkly could have told her otherwise. Vicky herself had been the problem; now it was the smoke, like torn dirty cotton bouncing off the yellow bluffs. The Apaches were the problem, now that Vicky was being reasonable.

When Phil was eleven, he and Donovan had visited the Esmeralda Mine, which Donovan partly owned. A splinter band of Ojo Caliente Apaches, raiding with Chiricahuas, under Cochise, had attacked the mine. Phil still carried a rib scar from that day, and on the way out they had passed two small ranches where embers smoked in the reek of mutilated death. Once through something like that, nerve-knotting memories forever knew the meaning of the Apaches.

When he returned to the walled rear yard, Donovan's sweeping scrutiny noted the Wells Fargo man standing watch on the station roof, and the elegant Tucson gambler on top of an open horse shed where he could look over the back wall.

The scant list of able-bodied men ticked again through Donovan's mind. Himself and Phil, Leeds and Wells Fargo, Kister, Stofer, and the Mexican hostler, Lieutenant Tuckerman and the gambler, and the raw-boned rancher out front and a younger cowman who'd come with him. Eleven men. An optimist might add Judge Elkins and three actors, one with long white hair and a half-filled whiskey tumbler constantly in one lean hand. Also the badly wounded teamster. Today Donovan was not an optimist. They were short on rifles, revolvers, and ammunition.

Tuckerman was still in the treetop when Donovan hopefully questioned Bill Leeds. "Troopers anywhere near?"

"Wisht I knew," Leeds admitted. "That Mex' kid from Dry Creek clumb up there, an' claimed he seen a flash over toward Keene Cañon Station, twenty-two mile. The Gen'ral went up with the wash mirror." Then, deadly serious, Leeds dourly advised: "Too quiet out there. Better pick your gun."

On a square of weathered canvas under the tree, Stofer and his hostler were laying out the station's lean arsenal—three revolvers, four rifles, a saloon shotgun, and boxes of shells, some of the boxes half empty.

Donovan stepped over and picked up the shotgun, a Lefever double-barreled hammer gun, sawed-off. The shells he scooped into coat pockets held buckshot, which was why he took the Lefever. He was testing trigger pull when Tuckerman's annoyed—"Damn tree won't stay still! Thought I saw something!"—floated down. Then Tuckerman's jubilant: "There it is! I see. . . ."

What Tuckerman saw was gulped by the brittle shatter of glass, which pelted down through the gray-green foliage. Tuckerman followed, all the way, crashing, flailing through the branches. His body geysered dust off the baked earth and subsided limply. Not now that first command for Second Lieutenant Tuckerman, or even "died in action"—whoever heard of the cavalry fighting in a treetop on some lonely forsaken flat? In Donovan the rest of it thrust like a hot wire. They were ten now. *Ten.*

The mirror frame, dark walnut with a rough wood backing, bounced near Donovan's feet, and Tuckerman's death was there. "Bullet holed his mirror!" Donovan called warning, and thought how easily it might have been Vicky, beside him on the road a few minutes ago.

Then Wells Fargo, on the roof, shouted: "Comin' outta the arroyo! They sneaked in close under the cutbanks!" His Remington repeater punched at the first wild chorus of howling threat as Donovan ran into the station.

Nothing, ever, was heroic about an Apache. He came in screaming surprise, and stank of grease, wickiup dirt, and animal habits. Coarse black hair was stringy and white cloth headbands dirty. He wore breechclouts and an occasional stolen shirt or pair of pants, and he killed with grisly blood lust.

In the front room's confusion, the solemn little girl with honey braids huddled against her mother's skirts and sought Donovan's ruddy face, which so recently had smiled reassurance.

Years ago, the first ranch below the Esmeralda had had one small girl like her. Phil had wept for miles with a boy's retching horror of what the Apaches had left. Donovan's own frozen rage haunted him now with the promise he had smiled at this small girl.

The raw-boned guard dashed in and barred the door. "Thirty, forty . . . mebbe more."

The elderly actor, silvery hair grandly back to his velvet coat collar, was peering in frozen fascination through a front window, whiskey glass forgotten in his hand. But no town hotel lobby this, with a street brawl outside. This was Cottonwood Station, on the Tucson road, and a musket muzzle smashed the window glass and its vomiting report blew half his face back through the room.

Women shrieked, and Donovan thought—*Still ten of us!*—as he lunged past the collapsing body and sighted a dark face behind the withdrawing musket barrel. The Lefever's answer shook the whole room. Donovan put the second buckshot load into a greasy breechclouted figure running past the window and had balm for his mounting rage. Even an Apache could appreciate the butchery of sawed-off buckshot, close up.

He was re-loading fast when Phil spoke at his elbow. "Need your Smith and Wesson?"

Phil's baggage held only his shiny new scalpels of mercy, and mercy had left Cottonwood Station this brassy midday hour. The full knowledge was in Phil's stony calm as he took Donovan's seldom-worn belt and revolver.

"Get the women into the kitchen!" Donovan ordered.

Glass from all three front windows quickly littered the floor. Phil fought one window, the raw-boned rancher the farther one. In the bedroom, a bearded, barefoot man, wearing overall pants, his bare torso bandaged, prowled with revolver gripped in one big hand. Phil's teamster patient was out of bed, guarding the lone side window in there. *Eleven men now.*

The whole long yard wall out back seemed under attack, and no help for the front room. Donovan turned his head when a ball of fire soared through Phil's window. It was bundled cloth, landing lightly on the broad floor planks and gushing yellow flames.

Phil jumped to stamp out the fire, and an arrow flicked lightly through his left shoulder and stopped there, protruding far out the back. A second fire mass came through

Donovan's window, rolling lightly on the floor in a stench of coal-oil flame.

Donovan drove buckshot through the window in greater fury. He guessed now what was coming. Reservation Indians knew coal oil. From some raided ranch, they had brought lamp oil to burn out the station. Sweating now, Donovan slid the overturned pine table over onto the oily blaze.

Phil was scorching shoes and trousers stamping out his fire. But Donovan's narrowed gaze fixed on the Boyd girl, at Phil's side now. She carried a small, silver-mounted Derringer, and her other hand was catching at the bobbing arrow shaft still protruding from Phil's shoulder. Her lithe body braced against Phil, and she pulled hard, quick, and brought the shaft on through, while Phil stood rigidly for the moment, his face set.

She dropped the arrow. Her wide skirts swirled with the quickness of her turn toward Phil's window with the small pocket gun. Phil's quicker hand hauled her back and roughly faced her toward the kitchen. His anger was a visible force.

Senetra Boyd made a helpless gesture and obeyed, and something that had been Donovan's life went from him. Against the Apaches he was one of eleven; after that, he was alone. For Phil's glower at the Boyd girl's back was built on angry fear for something cherished.

Smoke was lazily sifting in around the heavy front door. Donovan swore at the blue-gray drift, and went to Phil. "They'll be in quickly now!"

Phil eyed the door. A dark torment of agreement clouded his nod and quick look toward the kitchen doorway. The Boyd girl had stopped there and was watching them. Behind her shoulder, Vicky watched, too.

Futility stalked dismally through Donovan. *Too few guns.*
The Apaches were cunning now, quiet, avoiding window
openings, waiting for an entrance to burn through, and smoke
and fire to work inside. Then the screaming rush, the rich hot
bloody slaughter. It usually worked. Today it would work.

Donovan said: "Keep them out of the windows!"

Men were on top of the open front horse shed in the rear
yard and thinly scattered about the stages and wagons,
watching the wall rim. Beside Lieutenant Tuckerman's
body the gambler lay in his final indifference. The long-
faced young cowman had a sodden red bandanna around
his head. The yard gate was smoking, and fire outside
swirled sparks high above the wall.

Donovan gestured Stofer, Bill Leeds, Joe Kister around
him. These were the hard core, along with Wells Fargo, still
on the roof. The three listened to him, and Bill Leeds dryly
reminded: "Stofer, they always shoot high . . . an' you're
tallest. Donovan, wait fer all of us!"

In the long front room, smoke drifted in heavy gray
layers as Donovan went to Senetra Boyd. Vicky was still
with her, and Donovan looked at Vicky a moment before he
spoke to the girl.

"I'm going to open the front door. Want to say good bye
to Phil?"

Instant, understanding misery filled her look at Phil's
back. Vicky looked, too, and her pallor was a mask, strained
at nostrils and mouth corners, with helpless despair dark-
ening her blue eyes. Donovan remembered well that deep
clear blue of Vicky's eyes. She'd been sixteen then, in Phila-
delphia, and in all they'd planned, there had been no such
thing as naked Apaches outside the burning door of a place
called Cottonwood Station, or, for that matter, no long
years apart.

The Boyd girl's eyes were hazel under the black brows, and she was young enough to strike out passionately at what Donovan expected. "I won't say good bye! Why open the door?"

Donovan spoke past her to the despair in Vicky's look. For some reason now, he wanted Vicky to understand. "They'll be in anyway when the door burns through."

Vicky's very slight nod understood, and Senetra Boyd's hazel eyes widened as she listened to Donovan's undeniable familiarity with Mrs. Blassingham.

"Vicky, block off the kitchen doors! If you're sure there's no hope. . . ." Donovan indicated the Boyd girl's small gun. "Don't hesitate, Vicky! You must not let them take you. Believe me, if you ever did!"

"Yes, Mark," Vicky promised.

Donovan hesitated, and Vicky's old acute perception read his thought. Vicky shook her head.

"It won't help now, Mark. Don't tell him."

In a way it was easier than waiting. Only buckshot might do what Donovan hoped. Only buckshot, only Donovan. Accept that, and what else mattered, or had ever mattered? When Donovan was found outside, and Phil, too, probably, who had gained since Phil was three? The thought held Donovan for a moment while he waited at the door.

He wanted to look at Phil, touch the wounded shoulder; queerly, too, he wanted to turn back and tell Vicky again that this had to be tried. Instead, Donovan put two buckshot shells between his teeth, to be snatched fast to the Lefever's breech, if he had luck. With luck he could fire four times, at least, with the sawed-off shotgun. Then Bill Leeds and Phil and the others could keep on.

The men were banking up behind him, their guns ready. The raw-boned rancher reached for the door bar. His great yank hauled the door open. Flame and smoke gushed off the outside face of the door. Blazing brush collapsed in the doorway, and Donovan plunged through in a great spew of sparks and embers.

Greasy copper figures at his left started out of huddled waiting against the rough brown adobe wall. They had been watching the windows and roof edge above, bows strung and muskets cocked, but not watching for Donovan's lunge through the piled fire at the doorway.

The sawed-off Lefever drove buckshot down the line of startled figures, one barrel—two barrels. The shells between Donovan's teeth jammed home to the smoking breech. Again the Lefever fired two shattering reports.

Startled himself at what had happened, Donovan counted only three of eight or nine figures upright now, and those trying frantically to get around the station corner to safety. One staggered, one limped, and a rifle blurted at Donovan's shoulder and dropped that one.

Bill Leeds had fired the shot. Leeds jerked a suggestive thumb back the other way. Donovan swung around, reloading again.

A musket shot and two arrows had missed him. The men on the other side of the doorway blaze hadn't been so lucky. Donovan caught a glimpse of women inside the doorway beating at the burning wood with blankets. Arrows had dropped the raw-boned rancher, and just beyond him Phil was hunkered down, reloading the Smith and Wesson revolver. The teamster, still barefooted and bandaged, had backed against the adobe wall and was shooting from there.

Stofer was down. The other men were scattering out. They had killed five or six Apaches, and twice that number had retreated and fanned out at the corner of the station. Donovan's buckshot had a good spread when it reached them. The other guns were firing, too. Five Indians were dodging back past the corner of the station as Donovan ran forward, reloading once more.

They must be new to buckshot! he caught himself thinking, and it was a satisfying thought, seasoned with old memories of the Esmeralda raid.

Then at the building corner he saw the fire leaping and gnawing at the yard gate, and more of the dark, greasy figures all along the yard wall, where they had been waiting for the gate to burn through. How many, Donovan didn't estimate.

The long reach of high adobe wall gave him his guideline, and the targets were strung out along it. Donovan remembered Indians always shot high, and dropped to a knee as the nearest ran at him. He could see the lean flicking arrows, and their guns and revolvers hastily discharged, and he could see how his own buckshot ran its blade-like double bursts through them, dropping, crippling.

They don't like buckshot! he thought again. His twin sawed-off barrels reached out at fleeing backs as Phil and Joe Kister and others ran past him. Then, suddenly, it was surprisingly quiet and there was nothing to shoot at. The Apaches who could run had fled around the back wall, where they could reach the cover of brush.

They won't be back, Donovan thought, eyeing the greasy figures that hadn't got away, and some twenty minutes later he was certain of it.

The Wells Fargo man called from the station roof: "Dust this side of Prospect Rock! Eleven mile! Must be cavalry!"

Heading into the station then from the back yard, Donovan heard Bill Leeds make amends to the weathered tarp someone had thrown over Second Lieutenant Tuckerman.

"Gen'ral, I'll wave 'em down, an' mighty glad to see 'em," Leeds said.

Vicky's calm nod accepted the news when Donovan brought it to her in the long front room, still reeking of smoke.

"Mark, can you sit down now and drink that cup of coffee?"

Donovan's wry smile recalled the coffee.

"I need it," he admitted.

He watched Vicky walk to the kitchen. He saw the small girl with the honey braids. Her shy smile of belief made Donovan strangely content inside. The pine table had been put back upright. Others were sitting at one end. Donovan's foot dragged a hide chair where he could see, across the table and length of the long room, into the bedroom, which had become, in a way, Dr. Donovan's first office, with patients waiting.

After a moment Donovan reached out and pulled a second chair close. He watched to see if Vicky would bring coffee for herself, as she always had in the old days. When Vicky stepped out of the kitchen, carefully holding a mug in each hand, Donovan sat motionless, watching her.

Vicky took the chair he had placed close. "It should be stronger," she apologized, "but no one was thinking very clearly when it was made."

Donovan absently gulped the hot dark brew. "It's good." He watched Vicky looking across her untasted coffee to the bedroom doorway and said: "A busy first day for any doctor. That girl must have a strong stomach."

"She wants to help him," Vicky said, as if that explained everything.

"Well, it's their business," Donovan said. He caught Vicky's sideward appraisal of his meaning and lifted his coffee mug and then put it down. He asked, without looking at her: "Was there ever a divorce?"

Vicky's silence drew out, until her murmur reminded: "I died, Mark. Remember?"

Donovan remembered all of it, and some great grace shaped his words while he also watched the two busy figures in the bedroom.

"Home is a big empty house, Vicky, but they'll be near. Would you ever have me back?"

When Vicky finally spoke, her murmured reply had some small mirth and enduring understanding. "Thank you, Mark, for saying it that way." She looked at him, blue eyes level. "What do you think?"

About the Author

T. T. Flynn was born Thomas Theodore Flynn, Jr., in Indianapolis, Indiana. He was the author of over a hundred Western stories for such leading pulp magazines as Street & Smith's *Western Story Magazine*, Popular Publications' *Dime Western*, and Dell's *Zane Grey's Western Magazine*. He lived much of his life in New Mexico and spent much of his time on the road, exploring the vast terrain of the American West. His descriptions of the land are always detailed, but he used them not only for local color but also to reflect the heightening of emotional distress among the characters within a story. Following the Second World War, Flynn turned his attention to the book-length Western novel and in this form also produced work that has proven imperishable. Five of these novels first appeared as original paperbacks, most notably *The Man from Laramie* (1954) which was also featured as a serial in *The Saturday Evening Post* and subsequently made into a memorable motion picture directed by Anthony Mann and starring James Stewart, and *Two Faces West* (1954) which deals with the problems of identity and reality and served as the basis for a television series. He was highly innovative and inventive and in later novels, such as *Night of the Comanche Moon* (Five Star Westerns, 1995), concentrated on deeper psychological issues as the source for conflict, rather than more elemental motives like greed. Flynn is at his best in stories that combine mystery—not surprisingly, he also wrote detective fiction—with suspense and action in an artful balance. The psychological dimensions of Flynn's Western fiction came increasingly to encompass a confrontation with ethical principles about how one must live, the values that one must hold dear above all else, and his belief that there must be a balance in all things. The cosmic meaning of the mortality of all living creatures had become for him a unifying metaphor for the fragility and dignity of life itself. *Outlaws* will be his next **Five Star Western**.

FLYN
Flynn, T. T.
Reunion at Cottonwood
 Station

Dover
Public
Library

45 South State St.
Dover, DE 19901

Libraries Change Lives

DEMCO